Mystery of the ISLAND JUNGLE

Lee Roddy

FOCUS ON THE FAMILY

PUBLISHING
Pomona, California

To the memory of Bessie McDonald,
who prayed for me every day for thirty years
before her prayers were answered

MYSTERY OF THE ISLAND JUNGLE
Copyright © 1989 by Lee Roddy

Library of Congress Cataloging-in-Publication Data

Roddy, Lee, 1921-
  Mystery of the island jungle / Lee Roddy
    p. cm. — (A Ladd family adventure)
  Summary: Twelve-year-old Josh Ladd's discovery in the Kauai jungle of a
Japanese World War II airplane and its pilot who doesn't realize the war is
over leads him on a race against time with a conniving foe.
  ISBN 0-929608-19-4 : $4.99
  [1. Hawaii—Fiction.] I. Title. II. Series: Roddy, Lee, 1921-
Ladd family adventure.
PZ7.R6My 1989
[Fic]—dc19   89-11837
                                                                CIP
                                                                 AC

Published by Focus on the Family Publishing, Pomona, California 91799.
Distributed by Word Books, Dallas, Texas.

Editor: Janet Kobobel
Designer: Sherry Nicolai Russell
Cover Illustration: Ernest Norcia

Printed in the United States of America

First Printing

89 90 91 92 93 94 95 / 10 9 8 7 6 5 4 3 2 1

CONTENTS

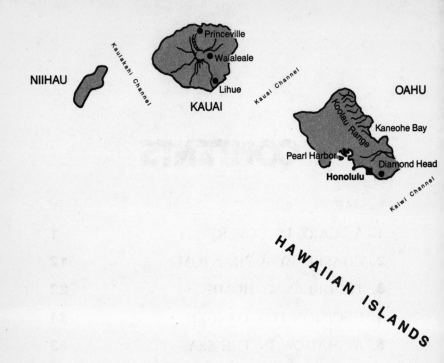

NIIHAU

Kaulakahi Channel

Princeville
Waialeale
Lihue

KAUAI

Kauai Channel

Koolau Range

OAHU

Kaneohe Bay

Pearl Harbor
Honolulu
Diamond Head

Kaiwi Channel

HAWAIIAN ISLANDS

Pacific Ocean

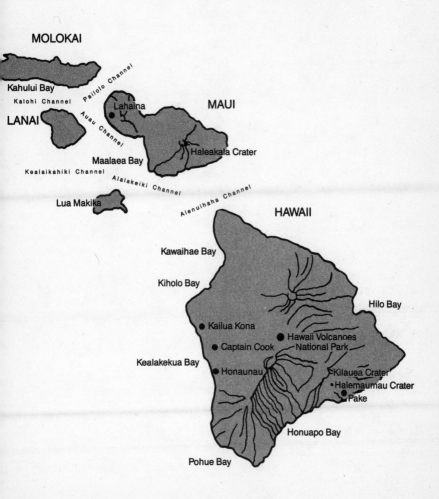

Pacific Ocean

MOLOKAI

Kahului Bay

Kalohi Channel

Pailolo Channel

Lahaina

MAUI

LANAI

Auau Channel

Maalaea Bay

Haleakala Crater

Kealaikahiki Channel

Alalakeiki Channel

Lua Makika

Alenuihaha Channel

HAWAII

Kawaihae Bay

Kiholo Bay

Hilo Bay

● Kailua Kona

● Hawaii Volcanoes National Park

● Captain Cook

Kealakekua Bay

● Honaunau

Kilauea Crater

● Halemaumau Crater

● Pake

Honuapo Bay

Pohue Bay

Chapter One

A SCARY DISCOVERY

Joshua Ladd was in trouble, but he wasn't alone. "We're lost!" he thought. Perspiring freely, his heart beating hard, he turned in the humid rain forest to look back at his two friends. Tank Catlett and Roger Okamoto puffed along a narrow trail made by wild boar, black-tailed deer, and wild dogs. All three boys wore basketball shoes, cutoff jeans, and tee shirts.

Twelve-year-old Josh called, "Hey, you guys!" He pushed a trailing banyan tree* vine out of the way. "It's getting late. We'd better get back to the helicopter." Josh was broad shouldered, with brown hair that curled away from his face.

Tank, Josh's long-time best friend, brushed the end of his sunburned nose with a deeply tanned hand. "I was thinking the same thing," he said in his slow, almost-drawling manner. Tank was also twelve but slightly

---

*The definition and pronunciation of words marked by an asterisk are contained in a glossary at the end of the book.

heavier than Josh, with blond hair bleached almost white by the sun.

Josh raised his blue eyes to thirteen-year-old Roger, bringing up the rear. "Hurry up, Rog!"

The third generation Japanese-American nodded, then suddenly stopped and stiffened. "Shh!" he hissed, cocking his head. He was slender as a wire and had copper-colored skin. Very black hair stuck straight out over his ears.

"What'd you hear?" Josh called softly.

Roger didn't answer. He turned slowly in the narrow trail, brown eyes probing the heavy foliage.

Josh and Tank also looked and listened, holding their breaths. The dense jungle trees, trailing vines, and high undergrowth made it difficult to see more than a few feet in any direction.

Overhead, the sun was hidden by the spreading green canopy. A lone shaft of sunlight made mottled shadows on the jungle floor. Myna birds and barred doves called in the distance, but otherwise there was silence.

The boys were on the remote, unexplored slope of a massive, extinct volcano called Mount Waialeale* on the island of Kauai,* Hawaii. Josh had learned since his family's recent move to the islands that the mountain is the world's wettest spot, receiving between 500 and 600 inches of rainfall annually.

After a moment, Roger shrugged and hurried on up the trail. He almost tripped over a huge, exposed banyan tree root. He caught his balance and jumped over wild guavas* that had fallen to the ground. As the pear-colored fruit rotted in the warm, moist air, fruit flies rose in a buzzing cloud. Roger hurried past.

"Thought I heard someone," Roger explained as he caught up with the other two boys.

Tank scoffed, "You know there's nobody on this mountain but us!"

Roger challenged, "How about the phantom Mr. Slayton told us about?"

Josh laughed. "He was just telling stories to entertain the girls while he flew us over here." Tiffany Ladd and Marsha Catlett were Josh's and Tank's older sisters. They had remained at the helicopter, which had landed in a clearing by a small body of water, while the boys explored the jungle.

Roger asked, "What about the stories Mr. Slayton told about clothes and food and tools and other stuff disappearing from people's houses?"

"That was down below, not up this high on the mountain."

Roger frowned. "A friend at school has grandparents who live on Kauai. They say there are ghosts in this place!"

Josh said firmly, "There are no such things as ghosts!"

"Maybe not," Roger said without conviction, "but I thought I heard something just now." He turned and looked the way they'd come. "Sounded like a person moving through the brush."

"Maybe it was a wild boar!" Tank exclaimed, his eyes widening in alarm.

"I don't think so," Roger replied. "Those mean hogs don't have to be quiet. They can cut your legs to ribbons with their tusks. Besides, what I heard was kind of sneaking, like a person who doesn't want to be seen."

"Well," Josh mused, "we know it couldn't be a man, because this is unexplored, primitive land. Mr. Slayton told us that probably nobody's ever been here before."

Roger shrugged. "Maybe it was a friendly little menehune.* Anyway, let's get out of here."

Josh nodded and looked around. He didn't want to admit to his friends that they were lost. He turned to Tank and said, "You want to lead the way back?"

"Not me. I'm worn out from breaking trail to this spot. Hey! Look!" Tank suddenly squatted and looked closely at the jungle floor. "Do they have bears on this island?"

Roger smiled. "No bears. No lions or tigers, either."

"Just the same," Tank replied, "that track was either made by a bear—or a man!"

Josh and Roger instantly bent to look at the place where Tank pointed.

"It's neither," Tank decided, standing again. "Just the way the light hits. That's all."

"Maybe so, Bruddah,*" Roger said, straightening up. "But moah bettah we go wikiwiki! Da kine jungle drive me pupule!"*

Roger could speak English very well, but like most Hawaiian kids, he sometimes used Pidgin English.* It was understood by the people of all the different cultures and ethnic backgrounds who lived in the fiftieth state.

Josh lifted his eyes to the soaring canopy of rain forest overhead. He couldn't see the sun to get his bearings. He turned to Roger and said, "How about you? Want to lead us back to the chopper? Tiffany and Marsha will worry if we're much later."

"No, thanks." Roger glanced nervously behind them.

Josh took a deep breath and decided. "Let's go back the way we came."

Roger protested, "Past where I heard—"

"It was probably just a deer!" Josh interrupted. "Anyway, that's the way I'm going."

Tank and Roger followed Josh single file down the trail until they came to the spot Josh thought they had entered it. Then he plunged into the trackless jungle, away from the trail.

He'd gone only a few feet when he stopped. "Those spiders!" he muttered, stooping to pick up a long tree limb from the jungle floor. The webs were about eight feet tall and six feet wide. They were occupied by black spiders with yellow bellies. Each spider was the size of a fifty-cent piece with legs.

As Josh swung the stick, knocking down a web, Roger said, "The spiders haven't had time to build those webs since we came by. That means we didn't come this way before." He paused, then asked softly, "Are we lost?"

Josh still didn't want to admit that. Instead, he pointed his spider stick off to the right. "There's a little more light over there, and it'll be easier going if we can get out of this rain forest and into an open area."

He added silently to himself, "And it'll be easier for the helicopter to find us if we can't find our way back."

"Watch out for the snails," Tank cautioned, falling into place behind Josh.

Josh nodded, stepping carefully so as not to crush the six-inch-long African snails that now seemed to be everywhere underfoot. They had beautiful shells, but the boys knew better than to touch them. Hawaiian residents won't even put a blade of grass into their mouths because the snails carry a liver fluke.* If their tiny eggs get into the body and hatch, they can damage a person's liver.

"I'm glad there're no snakes in these islands," Josh muttered. He pushed ahead, shoving ti* plants out of the way.

A stray shaft of sunlight penetrated the canopy. Josh caught a flash of silver off to his left. He stopped and stared into the tangled rain forest. "Wonder what that is?" he said.

The boys came up behind him, panting from the exertion of pushing through the dense foliage. Tank said, "Just a high mound of vines, ti plants, and things."

"No," Josh answered, pointing. "Stand where I am and

you'll see what looks like a sunbeam reflecting off of metal."

"Any metal in this jungle would be too rusted to reflect light," Tank reminded him.

Roger disagreed. "Not if it's aluminum."

Suddenly interested, all three boys shifted position until they all saw the reflection.

Josh said, "Let's go see." He carefully approached a mound of vines, wild ginger, and exposed tree roots. Tank and Roger followed single file. Except for one tiny point of reflected sunlight, there was only a pile of green. When Josh got closer, he pulled vines and leaves away. His fingers touched metal.

"Hey!" His voice rose in excitement. "It looks like it might be an old plane wreck." The boys had seen both military and civilian aircraft that had crashed into the jungles of the Koolau Range* behind Honolulu, where they lived. Excitedly, they began pulling and pushing the jungle growth back from their find.

Josh cried, "It's the fuselage of a plane! See? Must'a been here a long, long time, the way it's almost totally covered."

Suddenly, Roger stopped brushing at the tangled mass of plant and metal. "Uh-oh!"

"What?" Josh and Tank asked together.

"See that insignia?" Roger asked softly.

Tank asked, "You mean that red ball? It's so faded it's almost gone."

All thoughts of being lost or late returning to the helicopter had vanished from Josh's mind. His voice rose in excitement: "I recognize that from my father's history books! That's the rising sun emblem of Japan! This plane must've crashed here after attacking Pearl Harbor at the start of World War II!"

Josh's father was a former history teacher who had recently moved his family from Los Angeles County to Hawaii. He now published a small, weekly, tourist newspaper.

Tank protested, "That's impossible! That happened about fifty years ago!"

Roger shook his dark head. "Pearl Harbor's only about a hundred miles from here, so this plane could've been involved in the attack. Anyway, regardless of how it got here, it sure is a single-engine Japanese fighter plane! I think it was called a Zero!"

Tank exclaimed, "Josh, this'd make a great story for your father's newspaper!"

Josh made an annoyed gesture, striking the air with his closed fist. "I shouldn't have left my video camera in the chopper!"

Tank teased, "You were the one who said the camera was too awkward to carry into the jungle."

Josh gave his best friend a playful shove on the shoulder. "If I had it, I could probably sell some footage to that new television guy who moved into our apartment building."

"You mean Hotdog?" Tank asked. The newcomer from Los Angeles was boastful, so the kids called him by the nickname they gave to show-off surfers.

"His real name's Greg Grayson," Josh corrected. "He once told me he'd not only pay me if I got some good footage—if it's really good—but he'd also get it on the cable news networks. They buy from amateur news hounds."

Roger pulled at the brush. "So why'd you leave the camera with your sisters?"

"Quit talking and help me get this thing uncovered some more," Josh said, tugging at the vines and plants. "Hey! I know what!"

"What?" Tank asked as he pulled.

"I'll just have to get the camera and come back here! When I sell the tape, I'll have enough money to send for my grandmother! Dad can't afford to bring her over since he bought the paper. She's all alone now, and she's never seen Hawaii."

Tank and Roger kept working, knowing that Grandma Ladd had recently lost her husband. The couple's life savings had been used in an unsuccessful effort to save Grandpa Ladd's life.

Josh stopped tugging on a vine and faced his friends. "I just had a spooky thought: what about the pilot?"

Roger's superstitious nature made him draw back. "You mean—maybe his skeleton—"

Tank interrupted, "Roger, why don't you take a look

in the cockpit?"

"Not me, Bruddah!"

Josh said, "I'll look."

His two friends stopped working but stayed back while Josh picked his way carefully along the crushed fuselage. Standing on what remained of the left wing, Josh slowly stretched his neck as high as it would go. Without getting too close, he peered cautiously into the gloomy shadows of the vine-covered cockpit.

Josh's blue eyes skimmed the silent area where a man had once sat. The Plexiglas was gone. A giant snail oozed across the empty frame. A ti leaf sagged, then leaped. Josh drew back, heart pounding. He sighed in relief as a huge, black beetle scurried from the leaf to safety behind the instrument panel. Josh took a slow breath and turned back to face his friends. "Empty!"

Roger whispered, "Whew!"

Tank glanced around. "Then where is he? Unless he bailed out somewhere else, maybe his bones are right around—"

Suddenly, a terrible cry ripped through the jungle. "Banzai!"*

All three boys whipped around, their eyes straining to see into the jungle shadows. They instinctively drew back at the strange and terrifying sight before them. A short man with Oriental features crouched in the jungle trail. In spite of the humid heat, he wore a fur-lined flight jacket, high altitude pants, bright yellow boots, and a flying cap. He held a three-foot sword above his head.

"Banzai!" the figure shrieked, swinging the sword and charging toward the boys.

Roger whispered in awe, "The Phantom!"

Josh yelled, "Run!" He spun around and plunged blindly away from the fearsome sight of the swordsman.

Chapter Two

CHASED BY A PHANTOM

"**K**eep running!" Josh yelled to Tank and Roger without turning around. "Keep run—" His words were broken when his right foot caught in an exposed tree root and he crashed headfirst onto the jungle floor.

"Get up!" Tank shrieked, rushing toward him.

Josh had broken the fall with his hands, but he was slightly stunned. "I'm up!" Josh answered, staggering to his feet. He ignored the cuts and scratches on his hands, face, arms, and legs. Brushing a long ti leaf from his face, he ran on.

Roger panted from the rear, "That thing's still chasing us!"

Josh didn't look back, although he was subconsciously aware that Roger hadn't said "man." Josh kept running, stumbling, falling, leaping up, and staggering on again and again. He didn't know where he was headed, but he didn't care. All that mattered was escaping the weird figure chasing them with upraised sword. Josh moaned

12

an anguished prayer, "Oh, Lord! Oh, Lord!"

Along with the ragged breathing of his two friends, Josh thought he could hear those yellow boots thudding behind them. Their pursuer seemed to be gaining, but Josh didn't dare turn around to look. It was already hard enough to keep his balance.

Tank's usually slow voice gasped through labored breathing close behind Josh. "I—I can't go on much longer, Josh! My side's killing me, and my lungs are on fire!"

"Mine, too!" Josh replied, thrusting a vine the size of his arm out of the way. "But we can't stop now!"

"Hey, Bruddah!" Roger's voice broke with his exertion, but there was a note of hope in it. "Over there! To your left!"

Josh's anxious eyes swung that way. His heart leaped with hope. "I see it! A clearing! Hurry!"

He cut sharply to the left toward a break in the forest canopy. Moments later, he stumbled out of the jungle and into a small, grassy area. His hopes soared, then plunged sickeningly.

In the middle of the clearing was a crack in the earth about twenty feet across and running the entire width of the area. Josh slid to a stop at the edge and peered down the lava cleft. It was like a deep V with steep, black sides. A small body of water, like a tiny sapphire, lay to the left at the bottom.

Josh swallowed hard as Tank and Roger weakly panted

up beside him. Josh moaned and pointed. "Must be five hundred feet straight down!" He swiveled his head to look behind. He couldn't see the mysterious swordsman, but he could hear him crashing through the jungle after them.

"We're trapped!" Tank moaned, looking at the gorge before them. "There's no way we can jump that!"

Josh tore his eyes from the threat in the jungle and desperately glanced up and down the edge of the chasm. "Look!" he shouted.

He pointed to the right. About a hundred yards away, one tall banyan tree stood alone at the edge of the yawning fissure. The banyan trailed vines down from the limbs to the ground. Eventually, Josh knew, these would take root and support the tree's limbs. Some banyans could cover acres of ground that way.

What had caught Josh's eye were two slender vines that drooped like giant anacondas* from the high branches. They dangled about six feet off the ground. "Come on!" Josh yelled. He started running toward the solitary tree.

"You crazy?" Tank moaned. "He'll find us if we hide behind that tree!"

"We're not going to hide!" Josh answered, still running hard, ignoring the stitch in his side and the fire in his lungs. "Grab a vine and swing across!"

"Great idea, Bruddah!" Roger called.

Tank protested, "There're only two vines!"

"Each of you grab one, take a quick run, and then jump

across," Josh said. "The first one over throws a vine back to me!"

They were at the tree now, the supple vines tantalizingly close. Tank cried, "That guy'll get you before we can throw a vine back!"

"Don't argue!" Josh grabbed the nearest vine and shoved it into Tank's hands.

Tank gripped the vine and then shook his head. "No! We all have to go together!"

Roger reached out and seized the vine. "Dis vine hold planty* boys! Please kokua* everybody by jumping together!"

"I'll lead the way," Josh said, grabbing the smaller vine. With that, he ran a few quick steps away from the gorge, the vine in his right hand. Then he pivoted fast and ran hard toward the chasm, gripping the vine with both hands. "Here I go!"

Roger and Tank watched their friend as his body arched into the air. It swung like a clock's pendulum over the yawning cleft.

"Banzai!" The cry from the jungle's edge jerked both Roger's and Tank's eyes from Josh to the danger behind them.

"Grab the vine!" Tank yelled.

"Got it!" Roger replied hoarsely, seizing the remaining vine with both hands. "Ready?"

A moment later, the two friends ran hard toward the chasm, their hands on the vine. "Now!" Tank yelled.

They lifted their feet and arced into the emptiness above the gorge. Tank didn't intend to look down, but his fearful eyes darted to the ravine floor far below. It was a terrifying sight, with great chunks of ancient lava threatening destruction if they fell.

Tank jerked his eyes away from the danger below to focus on the far lip of the fissure. The grassy area on the other side seemed to stretch toward the boys as their weight carried them over the center of the chasm.

Suddenly, Roger realized something. "The vine's too short!" he yelled. "We're not going to go as far as Josh! Ready to let go?"

"Ready!" Tank cried as their shoes cleared the deep cleft and poised just inches over the far side.

Roger tensed, judging the distance. As the vine reached the farthest end of its arc and slowed, he could feel the vine start back toward the open fissure. He shouted, "Now!"

Both boys released the vine and dropped like stones. Tank landed on solid ground and rolled away from the chasm. Roger's right foot and most of his body landed on firm soil, but the cliff's edge gave way under his left foot. That threw him off balance. He started to slide backward into the chasm.

He grabbed desperately at the short grass, but there wasn't anything big enough to hold onto. His fingers dug frantically into the ancient volcanic soil, but his slide continued, faster and faster. Before he could yell, he felt

Josh's strong grip on his right wrist. A second later, Tank's hands clamped on his left wrist. With a quick, hard pull, Tank and Josh dragged Roger away from the danger.

"Thanks!" Roger gasped, leaping to his feet.

All three boys would have liked to collapse and rest, but they automatically turned to see where their strange pursuer was. Nothing could be seen except the lone banyan and the jungle. "He's gone," Tank whispered.

Roger was still breathing hard. He spoke between gulps of air. "Maybe. Maybe there wasn't anything there at all!"

Josh chided, "Now, Roger. You don't believe that. You saw him. We all did!"

"Yeah, Bruddah, but what did we see? The Phantom— or a ghost?"

Josh exclaimed, "That was a real person who chased us! A flesh-and-blood human being! Tell him, Tank!"

Tank brushed his hands and said nothing.

Josh urged, "Tank! Tell him! Tell—" He broke off his sentence. "Listen! Isn't that a helicopter?"

All three boys shaded their eyes and glanced upward. Josh saw it first. "It's ours! They're looking for us!" He began running and waving, shouting, "Hey! Here we are!"

"They've seen us!" Tank cried. "They're landing!"

The three friends ran toward the chopper as it eased to earth in the clearing. Josh asked, "What do you suppose they'll say when we tell them what we saw?"

Tank answered, "I hate to think!"

"Sure t'ing, Bruddah!" Roger agreed. "Those malihini* sistahs not going to believe one word we say!"

He was right. Josh's and Tank's older sisters didn't even wait for the pilot to help the boys back into the aircraft. "Where've you been?" Tiffany demanded from the front seat where she sat with Marsha and the pilot. All three wore large earphones. Tiffany didn't even give Josh time to answer. She pointed at him. "Look at you! Cuts and bruises and your clothes torn! What happened?"

The boys slid into the back seat with Josh behind his sister, Tank behind his, and Roger behind the pilot. Mr. Slayton sat on the right of the plastic bubble, which allowed maximum visibility.

Before Josh could answer, Marsha started in on Tank. "You realize how long you've been gone? We got scared and started looking for you! So you'd better have a good excuse, Tank!"

Clay Slayton, the chopper's tall, slender pilot, suggested, "You boys had better put on your headsets so you can hear. This baby's going to make a lot of noise until we're airborne."

The boys obeyed, slipping on the oversize earphones and snapping on their seat belts. The girls glared disapprovingly at them until the helicopter reached flying speed and leveled off, heading back to Princeville, the small farming community near Kauai's northwest coast.

When it was quieter in the cabin, Tiffany leaned

forward and frowned at her brother. At fourteen, she was inclined toward bossiness.

She spoke into the microphone that permitted everyone in the chopper to talk to each other above the steady throb of the overhead rotor. "You wait'll Dad hears about this! You scared us half to death being gone so long! And do you know how much it costs Dad per hour to charter this plane?"

"It's not a plane!" Josh replied, eager to tell about the old plane crash and the man who'd chased them. "Besides, Dad trades advertising space for the service, so it doesn't cost him—"

"Don't correct me!" Tiffany interrupted, giving her short, brunette hair an angry shake. "Don't you realize how frantic we were when you disappeared into that jungle and didn't get back? Don't you?" Her voice rose with each sentence.

Marsha chimed in, directing her fury at Tank. "You deserve to be grounded forever because of what you did!"

"Aw, Marsha," Tank protested. "Wait'll you hear what happened!"

Marsha snapped, "We won't believe you anyway!"

Josh realized the girls were really reacting to their scare by showing anger. He said softly, "You're right, Marsha. You two probably won't believe what really happened."

"Tell us anyway!" Tiffany replied, folding her arms over her chest.

"Yeah!" Marsha added. "Try us!" She was shorter than

Tiffany, and they both wore jeans and tank tops. The girls were best friends, just as Josh and Tank were.

Josh looked at Tank and Roger. Tank was squirming uncomfortably. Roger rarely said anything when he was around girls.

"Well," Josh began, and then he quickly described what had happened, except he didn't mention being lost.

Both girls listened without interruption until Josh had finished. Tiffany turned around in the front seat so she could look into her brother's face. "Let me get this straight," she said. "While you boys were exploring in the jungle, you found the wreck of a fifty-year-old Japanese warplane."

All three boys nodded solemnly.

"And," Tiffany continued, "while you were inspecting this wreck, a short man in old-fashioned flying clothes—"

"And bright yellow boots!" Tank interrupted.

"With a sword!" Josh added.

Tiffany and Marsha exchanged glances and suppressed smiles. Tiffany said, "This—person—chased you, yelling 'Banzai!' until you all escaped over a gorge by swinging across on vines?"

Josh bobbed his head emphatically. "Then he disappeared!"

Tank and Roger nodded in agreement.

Tiffany again looked at Marsha, then turned toward Josh and snapped, "Nobody in his right mind would believe you!"

The pilot cleared his throat. "Excuse me, folks," he said, turning to look at the girls. "It's possible they're right. I think they've just run into what folks on Kauai call 'The Phantom.' "

Chapter Three

TROUBLES AT HOME

It was late when the kids arrived home. They all lived in a three-story, concrete block apartment building at the base of Diamond Head in Honolulu. Tank and Marsha lived on the first floor. Josh and Tiffany climbed the outside concrete steps to the Ladd apartment on the second floor. Roger went to the top floor.

Josh caught a whiff of spaghetti sauce through the open louvered window. He glimpsed his mother at the kitchen range. She was tall and slender, with black hair and a dimple in her left cheek.

"Hi, Mom!" Josh called through the window as he passed.

She glanced up and exclaimed, "Oh, Josh! Tiffany! Thanks for calling from Kauai. I'll turn off the range and be right out to hear what happened."

The boy knew it was going to be hard to tell his parents about this afternoon.

Josh and Tiffany stopped at the sliding screen door and removed their shoes. That summer, when the Ladd family had moved from California to Hawaii, their mother had bought an off-white rug she'd always wanted. To protect it, the family members had adopted the Oriental custom of removing their shoes before entering their home.

"That spaghetti sure smells good!" Josh said, sliding the screen door open for his sister and entering after her. Their father came out of the back bedroom wearing a robe. He was a nice-looking man, six feet tall, with dark, wavy hair. He peered over the top of silver-framed half-glasses he had only recently started wearing. "I'm glad you're home," he said. "Your mother and I were getting concerned."

Nathan, Josh's ten-year-old brother, bounded barefoot down the hallway from the bedroom the two boys shared. "Yeah! How come you're so late?"

Before Josh or Tiffany could answer, their mother walked out of the kitchen with a long-handled, wooden spoon in her right hand. She stopped suddenly with a sharp intake of breath. "Joshua! What in the world happened to you?" She rushed to the boy and quickly examined his cuts and bruises. "I'll get the first-aid kit."

He pulled away and shook his head. "Not now, please, Mom. I'm okay."

His father moved closer and looked down at Josh before asking, "Are you sure?"

"I'm sure."

Both parents seemed uncertain but turned to silently question Tiffany. She shrugged, so the parents accepted the boy's word. Mrs. Ladd gave Tiffany a quick kiss on the cheek and asked, "Could you all sit in the kitchen so I can listen?"

Her husband said mildly, "There's more seating room here in the living room, Dear. Can't you leave your cooking for a few minutes?"

"No," she said. "There's a lizard on the ceiling right over my range, and I'm watching him."

Her husband said patiently, "I've told you, Mary, that's only a harmless little gecko."

"Oh, I'm not afraid of his biting me!" Mrs. Ladd explained. "I just don't want him to fall into the spaghetti."

"He won't fall," John Ladd assured her. He motioned to the tropical-print rattan couch and three matching occasional chairs. "Everyone please take a seat, and let's hear what happened."

Nathan, the family's youngest and small for his age, jumped backward onto the couch and exclaimed, "What tore up your face and hands like that, Josh?"

"Well," Josh began uncertainly, and then he stopped.

Tiffany jumped right in. "He claims to have found a Japanese World War II airplane crashed in the jungle." She paused dramatically and added, "He also says an old Japanese-looking guy in flying clothes chased him, Tank, and Roger with a sword."

"A sword?" Mrs. Ladd exclaimed. "Is that how you got hurt, Josh?"

"No, Mom! We all ran, so he never got close. I got

scratched up from running through the jungle."

John Ladd suggested, "Maybe you'd better tell us the whole story, Son."

Reluctantly, fearing his father would deny him any privileges for a while, Josh told about everything except getting lost. He hadn't told Tiffany or Marsha about that, either.

When he finished, Tiffany exclaimed, "See? It's a pretty wild story."

Josh replied with some annoyance, "The pilot believed it! He thinks it might have been what the locals call The Phantom."

Tiffany said with a disdainful sniff, "But Mr. Slayton also said nobody's ever seen this phantom before. They've just had things disappear, like food and clothes and tools, so they blamed it on a phantom."

"They have so seen him!" Josh replied.

"Only from a distance," Tiffany argued. "Sort of like Big Foot in the western United States and the Abominable Snowman of the Himalayas. But there's no proof any of them exist."

Nathan asked, "What's a phantom?"

"Something like a ghost," Tiffany said. "Only there aren't any such things."

"I didn't say it was a ghost!" Josh protested.

Nathan shook his dark hair. "Roger says there are ghosts. So do Kong and some of the other kids."

Josh grimaced at the mention of Kamuela* Kong, whom

the kids called King Kong behind his back. He was the neighborhood bully.

Mr. Ladd said, "Keep your voices down! You know how sound carries through this building. Nathan, let's understand the difference in what your brother and sister are talking about." The father's voice took on a schoolteacher tone. "A phantom is a person or thing that's merely illusionary; an appearance without real substance. You understand?"

"I think so," Nathan replied.

"And a ghost is the soul or spirit of a dead person that seems to appear to living people. However, there are no such things as ghosts."

Nathan asked, "But there are phantoms?"

John Ladd frowned. "Well, in the sense that they aren't real. A phantom is an illusion, apparition, or wraith."

Tiffany protested, "Dad, are you saying something did chase them?"

"Look at your brother's face and clothes. All three boys saw the same thing and ran. I'm simply trying to figure out who it might have been."

His wife asked, "And who do you think it was?"

"It had to be a man, but who he was and why he chased the boys is a mystery. Who do you think it was, Josh?"

Josh shrugged. "I don't know, except he looked like pictures of those World War II Japanese fighter pilots you've got in your old history books."

His father took off his half-glasses and chewed on an

earpiece. Then he pulled a neatly folded white handker-
chief from his right rear pants pocket and absently
polished the lenses before answering. "Then you think
it was really a man?"

Josh nodded. "The sword was real, too."

"How do you explain the high altitude flying clothes
in that humid jungle?"

"I don't know, Dad, but that's what he was wearing."

"Do Tank and Roger agree with you?"

"Yes, except Roger thinks it was a ghost. Tank's not
sure."

Mr. Ladd nodded. "Some locals are quite superstitious,
like believing in Pele,* goddess of the volcanoes."

Tiffany added, "And menehunes, those little people like
fairies or leprechauns."

Mr. Ladd took a slow breath. "Well, since it wasn't
any of those imaginary creatures, let's consider some
logical possibilities."

"Like what?" Josh asked.

"Well, Son, you've seen a lot of Japanese samurai warrior films at the Saturday matinee and on local television,
haven't you?"

"Yes." Josh didn't see what that had to do with anything.

"Those actors have sword fights, don't they?"

"Yes."

"And you've seen old World War II movies on TV with
Japanese planes. Right?"

"I've seen some," Josh admitted.

"And haven't Roger and some of his friends found old plane wrecks in these mountains before?" Mr. Ladd waved a hand toward Diamond Head. The ancient volcanic landmark sat massively in front of the Koolau Range. The green mountains ran along the inland side of Honolulu like a giant's backbone.

Josh nodded, still not knowing where his father was going with this line of questioning.

Mr. Ladd said, "You've already mentioned seeing my history textbooks with pictures of Japanese flyers from World War II."

"But Dad, those pictures are all in black and white, not color. This guy who chased us had on yellow boots."

"You forget, Son," Mr. Ladd continued softly. "Your grandfather told us all about the time when a kamikaze suicide plane crashed onto the carrier where he served during World War II."

Josh nodded. "I remember that."

The boy's thoughts jumped from their conversation to memories of his grandfather. The elderly man had recently died. Josh had been close to both sets of grandparents, but now that Grandma Ladd was alone, Josh wanted very much to bring her to the islands.

There was a terrible risk in doing that, Josh had learned by accident not long before. One still night when the trade winds weren't blowing, he'd heard his parents talking. In order to bring his mother over, John Ladd had applied to the bank for a loan. He had offered to put up his newly purchased tourist publication as security. That meant if he couldn't make the payments, the bank would foreclose and he'd lose the paper. Losing the paper might in turn force the Ladds to move back to the Mainland in search of work.

The worst thing about the situation to Josh was that if they left Hawaii, he'd again be separated from his best friend, Tank. Josh didn't want that to happen, so he had been trying to think of ideas to earn the money himself to bring his grandmother over.

Josh had told his parents about his plan, but he hadn't mentioned overhearing what a risk they'd be taking if the bank approved the loan. The decision was due in two weeks.

Josh told himself, "I've got to find a way to get the money for Grandma's trip before the bank approves the loan! But two weeks isn't much time."

The boy's mind snapped back as his father continued. "Son, do you also remember that your grandfather's most vivid memory of that incident was the pilot's yellow flight boots?"

Josh hadn't remembered, but the suggestion upset him. "Are you saying I put all those things together and made up this story?"

Mr. Ladd crossed to his son's side and laid a gentle hand on his shoulder. "I have no reason to doubt your word, Son. But your story is so unusual I just wanted to think of all logical possibilities."

"I've told you what happened, Dad."

"I believe you, Son. It's just too bad you didn't take some video footage of the plane."

"I should have," Josh admitted, "but I thought the camera would be too heavy to carry in the jungle. I left it in the helicopter."

"You know what we could do, Son?"

"What?"

"You could take me back there so we could shoot some tape."

Josh took a slow, deep breath. "I thought about it. I'd give you some of the stills* for your paper, then maybe I could sell the video tape to the cable networks. With the money, I'd bring Grandma over here."

John Ladd's jaw muscles twitched. "That's very nice of you, Son. I've been thinking a lot about flying her over since my father died, but your mother and I have sunk every dime we own into the newspaper. So cash flow is tight. Fortunately, I can trade advertising space for services like transportation on Clay Slayton's helicopter."

"I know, Dad."

"But if you found that wreck again—"

Josh interrupted, lowering his eyes. "I can't, Dad!"

"Why not?"

"We—I—got lost." He expected his confession would bring sharp reprimands from his parents.

His mother didn't seem to hear, however, for she suddenly jumped up and turned toward the kitchen. "I've got to check my spaghetti," she said.

After she left the room, her husband said, "So the real reason you were late is that you boys got lost?"

Tiffany exclaimed, "I should have guessed!"

Josh shot an annoyed glance at her but kept his head down.

"Son, don't you think you should have told us that first?"

Josh raised his eyes. "Yes, but finding the old plane and being chased was so exciting, I forgot! Besides, even if I'd had the camera, I was running so fast I'd never have shot any footage of him."

Suddenly, Mrs. Ladd shrieked from the kitchen, "He's gone!"

The rest of the family dashed into the tiny kitchen, calling out, "Who's gone?"

"The lizard!" Mrs. Ladd dropped her wooden spoon and snatched up two pot holders. In one swift motion, she scooped up the pot of spaghetti and dumped it into the garbage disposal.

Nathan cried, "Why'd you do that, Mom?"

"I'm not going to take a chance I cooked that lizard with my family's food!" She turned on the water and threw the switch. The disposal ground loudly. For a moment, the rest of the family stared in open-mouthed surprise. Then they looked at each other and started to laugh. They still had the giggles when they went out for hamburgers.

But Josh hadn't heard the last of The Phantom. The next morning at breakfast, his mother asked him to run down to the corner store and buy a quart of milk. Josh stepped into his shoes outside the sliding screen door, subconsciously hearing the calls of the Japanese barred doves from the eaves and feeling the warm trade winds on his face.

A man's voice called from the adjoining apartment, "Josh, wait up!" The boy stopped and waited. A handsome man in a tropical, striped, blue suit and coordinated tie stepped quickly through the sliding screen door. "Remember me, Josh?"

Josh nodded. He almost said, "Hotdog Grayson." Instead he said, "You're Greg Grayson, who won all those awards for television news in Los Angeles."

"Investigative reporter," the newcomer said with an artificial smile. "Specializing in controversial subjects." He bent and looked the boy in the eye. "It's all over the apartment building about that plane wreck and the old geezer with the sword who chased you boys yesterday. Take me there with a camera crew, and I'll slip you a few bucks."

Josh didn't much like the man, but he answered politely, "I don't know how to get back there."

Hotdog's smile changed slightly, but he still seemed friendly. "You wouldn't want one of your buddies to get paid instead of you, would you?"

The question annoyed Josh, but he kept his voice even.

"We were all lost, so they don't know how to get there, either." Josh turned and took the stairs down three at a time to the parking lot.

Hotdog yelled after him, "I'm going to find that plane and the old swordsman anyway!"

Josh thought, "I hope you don't!" just as he heard a yell from the yellow be-still tree* that grew at the edge of the parking lot.

"Hey, you! Haole* boy!"

Josh moaned inwardly, "Oh, no! That's King Kong!" He turned slowly, knowing he was in trouble.

Chapter Four

DECISION FOR DANGER

Josh's insides churned hard and seemed to twist into a knot at the sight of Kamuela Kong. "Hi, Kong," he said. They had met in a most unfortunate way shortly after Josh moved to Hawaii.

One morning, Josh and Tank had been exploring the junglelike mountains behind Honolulu. Tank had stopped to pick up some wild guavas while Josh continued around a curve along the narrow trail. Josh grabbed a vine trailing from the dense, overhead canopy of trees, then started to run, grasping the vine in both hands.

"Hey, Tank!" Josh called, coming to the end of the vine and sailing up into the air. "Watch me!" Josh was carried about fifteen feet through the air before he let go of the vine. He braced himself to land on his feet.

Instead, he was startled to see his basketball shoes aimed straight at the bare chest of a big local boy who had suddenly stepped out of the thick undergrowth. "Look out!" Josh yelled. It was too late. Josh's feet struck the kid right in the middle of his wide chest.

"Oof!" The stranger fell hard on his backside.

Josh managed to land on hands and knees. He jumped up fast. "You okay?" he asked, bending over the victim. Josh guessed the other boy weighed around 200 pounds and stood nearly six feet tall, although he couldn't have been more than thirteen years old.

For a moment, the huge stranger was stunned. He shook his head of black, curly hair. He had wide, flaring nostrils and deep brown eyes that slowly focused on Josh. Then he growled, deep in his throat, like an animal. "Hey, you haole boy! Why for you do dat, huh?"

At the time, Josh wasn't too familiar with Pidgin English, but he understood what the boy meant. "It was an accident!" Josh turned to point to the trailing vine he'd used to swing through the air. The vine still bounced from where it was anchored to a tree limb forty feet up. "See? I—"

He broke off as the big kid leaped to his feet with a roar. Josh took a step back as the stranger grabbed for Josh's neck.

"Hey, wait!" Josh exclaimed, dodging as best he could in the narrow trail. "I didn't mean to—"

Tank came calling around the curve, "What's going on, Josh? Uh oh!" Tank stopped.

The curly-haired local boy paused at the sight of Tank. Both Josh and Tank were big, with well-developed upper bodies, so the stranger considered the situation and decided he didn't want to take on two big boys at once.

He asked, "You live heah, Bruddah?"

Josh nodded and spoke rapidly, hoping to head off the stranger's anger. "Yes. Tank and I live right on the side of Diamond Head. In the apartments. He's lived here a long time, but I just moved here."

The big kid smiled slowly. He swept his hands in a broad gesture toward the jungle, the mountains, and on down toward where the Pacific Ocean was out of sight. "Dis all belong me—Kong!"

Josh blinked in surprise. "I thought this was public land. I mean, since this is the fiftieth state in the Union, and—"

"Belong me!" the boy interrupted with a shout. "You come heah again, you be sorry!"

Josh asked in disbelief, "What?"

"I already owe you one kick like you give me, Bruddah! I find you heah again, you both get planty pilikia!"*

Josh felt his insides churn with resentment. His stubborn tendency started to surface. "Now wait a minute—"

Tank's firm hand on his bare arm made Josh stop. His friend whispered, "Let's go!"

"I'm not going to—"

"Come on, Josh! Now!"

Something about Tank's insistence had made Josh yield. Wordlessly, he turned and followed Tank back down the trail toward home.

Josh muttered, "Who does he think he is?"

Tank whispered, "He's Kamuela Kong, that's who!

The neighborhood kids call him King Kong after the movie monster. He's part Hawaiian and part Samoan, but the rest is plain mean. He's the worst bully on the whole island, and he'll make life miserable for you!"

That experience had been a month ago, and Josh had since learned a lot more about Kong. Now Kong stepped away from the dense foliage of a be-still tree. One of the yellow flowers had dropped on his curly hair, but he didn't seem to notice. Josh didn't think it was funny.

He swallowed hard and said, "I'm on my way to the store for some milk. Can't stop!"

"Wait, Bruddah!"

Josh waited, knowing the Pidgin term for brother didn't mean anything to Kong. Josh tried to keep from showing his concern as the bully passed a clump of pink-blossomed oleanders* and stopped, his legs spread. Josh had never seen such wide, heavy feet. "I'm in a hurry," Josh repeated.

Kong held up a warning hand. "Wait, I said!"

Josh watched Kong raise the heavy, brown-skinned hand and run it along his hair. It grew wildly in every direction. The yellow be-still blossom fell unnoticed to the parking lot pavement. To Josh, Kong looked like a brown fire plug with legs, walking around on blue and white zoris.*

"Why for you bother dah ghost?"

The question surprised Josh. "Ghost?"

Kong waved a hand the size of a coconut. "In dah

jungle yesta'day."

Josh was surprised how fast the story had spread through the neighborhood by what was called the "coconut wireless." He said, "It wasn't a ghost, and we didn't—"

"Whadda you mean, 'not ghost'? You call Kong liar?"

"No, of course not! But—"

He broke off as a woman's voice called loudly from beyond the twenty-foot-tall growth of bamboo and oleanders at the edge of the apartment complex. "Kamuela!"

"Your mother's calling," Josh said with relief.

"Let her call!" Kong stirred uneasily, and Josh had the strange feeling that maybe this giant kid was afraid of his mother. Still, Kong wasn't going to let that be known. "You leave dah kine ghost alone! You make ghost huhu,* maybe so him hurt my relatives live on Kauai!"

"Kamuela!" The voice was louder and more firm.

Kong shrugged. "I was going home anyway." He turned away and called over his shoulder, "'Membah what I say, malihini!"

Josh nodded, wondering why Kong cared about disturbing something that didn't exist. But Josh was so glad Kong was leaving that he almost ran down the slight hill toward the corner store.

By nature, Josh was a fast-moving, fast-talking person. He ran through a flock of myna birds. The lazy, black imports from India would rather walk than fly. They scattered before Josh, hopping like kids in a sack race. Only one myna flew, showing a white patch on its back.

"That plane wreck's going to be nothing but trouble!" Josh told himself as he hurried along. "Why'd I ever have to—" He broke off his thought and stopped, sniffing the air. "Malasadas!"* he thought, licking his lips as he pictured the Portuguese pastry.

Josh turned to look at a small board and batten house.* It sat high off the ground to discourage termites. The corrugated tin roof was rusted from hard seasonal rains. In the front yard, banana trees rustled in the trade winds. The sweet fragrance of plumeria* blossoms mixed with the malasadas.

"Hey, Josh!" The boy turned toward the front screened porch. Manuel Souza's outline was barely visible. "Come in. My mom's just made malasadas," Manuel said enticingly, opening the screen door with his bare foot.

"I'm on my way to the little store."

"One quick malasada?" Manuel asked with a grin. He was thirteen, olive-skinned, and had dark, wavy hair. He wore long, print shorts without shoes or shirt.

Josh answered, "Well, okay, but I'll have to gobble it down." Josh turned from the street, pushed open the sagging, wire gate, and hurried up the short path to the door.

Manuel was considered very akamai* and was a top student in school. He held out a plate heaped with small, round pastries that looked something like doughnuts without a hole. "Take two. They're small," he offered.

Josh obeyed. "Mom'll be mad if I spoil my breakfast, but these are too good to pass up." He reached over and took two of the malasadas. The sugar coating fairly crackled as he lifted the first pastry to his mouth. "Umm! Your mother sure is a good cook!"

The boys leaned against the wooden posts that supported the porch's tin roof. Manuel said with a mouthful, "Tell me about the plane you guys found yesterday."

Briefly, Josh obeyed, marveling again at how fast word of the discovery had raced through the neighborhood. When he finished, Manuel offered him another malasada. He declined with a shake of his head. "I've got to get back for breakfast." He popped the second malasada into his mouth.

"You know what's going to happen?" Manuel asked, licking sugar off his fingers. "People are going to want to know everything about that plane and the pilot, or whoever the guy was with the sword. The locals will say you disturbed a ghost, and they won't like it."

"Kong already warned me about that, even though there aren't any ghosts."

"It's what people believe that's involved here."

Josh nodded thoughtfully, remembering when he and his sister had been caught in an erupting volcano on the Big Island of Hawaii. The locals were convinced that Pele, goddess of the volcanoes, had been huhu and caused the eruption.

"Sure wish I could have shot some footage of that plane with my video camera," Josh mused. "That'd prove the part was true about the crashed plane."

"Aren't you afraid of the man with the sword?"

"He scared me," Josh admitted. "Boy! I sure wish I'd shot some footage of him! But when I saw him running at me, yelling and with that sword raised...."

"Are you brave enough to risk going back there with your camera?"

"My father said he'd go with me, but I can't because I don't know how to find my way back. The three of us were lost when it happened."

"Couldn't you identify some landmarks?"

"I don't think so. It's all jungle. Nobody's ever been there before."

"How about Tank and Roger?"

"I don't see how they could, either."

"Sometimes if you stop and think carefully, you can remember things you didn't think you knew. Then you could draw a map. Get Tank and Roger to help you."

Josh thought for a moment. "That might work. There was this blue lagoon where we landed, and I remember a lava shaft like a spear point where we entered the jungle." His words came faster as he thought. "Then there was the lone banyan tree by the crevice where we swung across on vines. Yeah! That might work!"

"Then do it!" Manuel urged.

"Maybe I will. With what the chopper pilot could

remember, I might find that plane again! Then I'd give my dad some of the stills for his paper and sell the video tape to one of those cable or television networks. They'd probably pay me enough that I could bring my grandmother over. Except, well, what if The Phantom—or whoever he was—is still there?"

"Was The Phantom really guarding the plane?"

"I think it was a man, but I don't know why anyone would guard a wreck fifty years old."

"You'll be safe with your father, especially if Tank and Roger go along."

"I hope so."

"And if you don't solve the mystery, you can bet Hotdog's going to try."

"He's already working on it," Josh admitted. "He might be able to help sell my video tape to the networks, but I don't want him to beat me out of the story. Well, thanks for the malasadas. I've got to get going."

Josh ran down the street toward the little store. In spite of the eighty-degree heat, a shiver of fear tingled his spine. But he knew he had to go back to the rain forest, no matter what dangers he might face.

Chapter Five

A SHADOW IN THE SKY

After John Ladd had asked the blessing at breakfast, Josh briefly recounted his talk with Manuel. Then he announced his decision to find the wreck again.

His mother made a little startled sound. "Oh, Joshua!" she said. "What about the man with the sword?"

"Dad'll be with me. Maybe Tank and Roger. They can go if they want, can't they, Dad?"

John Ladd sipped his glass of pink guava juice before answering. "Of course, Son. Now, Mary, I don't think there's any real danger."

Nathan cried, "Can I go?"

"May I?" his mother corrected automatically. "And no, you may not. John, I wish you and Josh wouldn't go, either."

Josh took a spoonful of melonlike papaya* but stopped it in midair until he heard what his father would say.

His dad wiped his lips with a napkin and looked across the Formica-top table at his wife. "Listen, Dear. I believe whoever scared the boys was doing just that—scaring them. I doubt he would have hurt them. He certainly won't if I'm along."

"But you don't know that for sure, John."

"We'll be careful. It's a story worth following because it could be of national importance. Right now, our struggling little paper could use a top-notch feature and a little recognition. We might even be able to pull it out of the red."

"And then we could bring Grandma over, too!" Josh added quickly.

Mrs. Ladd started to protest again, but Tiffany spoke for the first time. "Oh, Mom, quit worrying. They'll be okay."

Josh turned surprised eyes on his older sister. He could never figure her out. Sometimes she was such a pain, and other times she was a great person. "Thanks, Tif," he said.

Their father set his empty glass on the table with finality. "Then it's settled. Josh, why not ask Tank and Roger to help you draw some kind of map? I'll call the helicopter office and arrange for Clay Slayton to fly us back to this lake where you landed."

"Blue lagoon," Josh said.

His father asked, "Lagoon? I thought it was back up in the mountain."

"It is," Josh said.

"Then technically it can't be a lagoon," Mr. Ladd explained. "A lagoon is a kind of shallow water, like a pond, close to the ocean."

Josh made an impatient gesture. "Pond, lake, lagoon. It doesn't matter except as a landmark to find the place we landed the chopper so we can start looking for the plane from that point. That's the only way to solve the mystery."

Mary Ladd finished her papaya and laid down her spoon. "I don't like the sound of it at all. But if you two insist on going, let's pray about it first. Okay?"

"Certainly," her husband replied, and then he led the family in a brief prayer asking for God's protection. Afterward he said, "Josh, you'd better get together with Tank and Roger."

"I'm ready," Josh said. "May I be excused?"

His parents nodded. Josh scooted his chair back and ran barefoot to the lanai.* Stepping outside, he barely noticed Diamond Head standing like a massive sentinel above the apartments. The famous landmark was brown and ugly with summer koa* and other growth.

Josh was aware the trade winds had died down. That sometimes happened, especially when a kona, or south wind, was likely to follow. Sometimes kona winds brought storms. Josh cupped his hands over his mouth and looked over the rail. "Hey, Tank!" he called.

A moment later, the sliding screen door below opened, and Tank's almost-white hair showed. He leaned over his lanai rail and looked up. "I heard! Be right up!"

"You heard what?" Josh asked in surprise.

"What your family said at breakfast." Tank grinned. "When the trades die down, everybody can hear everything that's said through these louvered windows."

"Yeah, Bruddahs!" Roger's face appeared at the third-floor lanai railing. "I heard, too! Come on up to my room! I've got paper and pencils for drawing a map!" Josh ran to the front door, slipped on his zoris, and slap-slapped upstairs to the Okamoto apartment. He stepped out of his zoris at the door, noticing that only Roger's shoes were there. Mr. and Mrs. Okamoto weren't home.

Josh had been in the Okamoto living room before, but never in Roger's bedroom. In the front room, Mrs. Okamoto had taught Josh and his family a few Japanese words. Roger's maternal grandmother, Masako Yamaguchi, had been born in Tokyo. She had married a Hawaiian soldier of Japanese descent when he was stationed there with American occupation forces after World War II.

Josh followed Roger out of the living room, which was filled with Japanese Kabuki dolls* Roger's Grandmother Yamaguchi had made. The two boys walked past shoji screens* and other Oriental decorations.

For a moment before stepping into his friend's bedroom, Josh wondered if Roger slept on a mat, Japanese style. He was surprised to see a regular bed under a large, louvered window. There were surfing posters on the wall, along with pictures of Japan's Mount Fuji and various scenic shots of Hawaii.

"Sit here," Roger said, indicating a plastic beanbag chair that seemed out of place. Josh glanced out another louvered window, seeing the strangely shaped leaves of a rubber tree plant above the top of the walkway that connected the various third-floor apartments.

"In a minute," Josh replied, looking around the room. He walked over to three small shelves on the wall directly across from the door. A tiny, Oriental-looking shrine with a covered urn sat on the lower shelf. "What's in the vase?" Josh asked.

"My Grandfather Okamoto."

Josh turned around with a grin, thinking Roger was teasing. "I mean really," Josh said. He turned back and reached out to remove the top.

"My grandfather's ashes," Roger said quickly.

Josh jerked his hand back as though he'd been bitten by a snake. He had often seen Asian cemeteries with coins, apples, paper notes, and other materials on the gravestones. He also knew that some bodies were not buried but cremated. This, however, was the first funeral urn he had ever seen.

Roger explained, "He was working at Pearl Harbor when the attack came. Later, he was interned on the Mainland with others of Japanese ancestry."

Josh turned, swallowing hard. Since the Ladds had moved to Hawaii, the family had studied the islands' history with new interest. Josh knew that in World War II, people like the Okamotos, although Americans, had been placed in what some called 'concentration camps' for fear they'd help Japan with espionage. Most of the Japanese-Americans were held for the war's duration without trial or even accusation. Yet there hadn't been a single case of Japanese-Americans doing anything to aid Japan.

Roger added, "He later volunteered and served with the 442nd. You heard of that?"

Josh nodded. John Ladd had made sure his family knew about Hawaii's famous "Go for Broke" soldiers. The Japanese-Americans in the outfit, mostly fighting in Italy against Germany and the other Axis* powers, had been awarded more medals than any other American fighting unit.

Josh looked at the urn again, thinking what it represented. "I'm sorry," he said softly.

"It's okay. He was wounded three times. Lost an arm. But after the war, he came back here and lived until two years ago."

Josh turned around, a strange lump rising in his throat. "I've been to the Pearl Harbor Memorial. Now I understand something about what happened that day in 1941 that I never thought about before. And both of your grandfathers fought for America during the war, one in Italy and the other in the Pacific."

"It was long before we were born." Roger changed the subject. "I've been thinking about that plane wreck, and I've made some notes." He indicated the desk just as

Tank knocked on the door.

Roger raised his voice. "We're in my room!"

A moment later, Tank padded barefoot down the hallway and joined the discussion about the map. Roger took the chair in front of the desk. He began to draw as the boys recalled landmarks in the jungles of Waialeale.

When the map was completed to each boy's satisfaction, Roger laid down his pencil and leaned back. "What do you guys think?"

"Perfect!" Josh said, pointing. "There's the blue lagoon where we landed, the spear point of lava where we entered the jungle—"

"And there's the tree we used to swing across the canyon!" Tank interrupted. "Now, what are some other landmarks we saw that will help us when we go back?"

Josh asked, "You're going with Dad and me?"

Tank shook his head. "My dad wants me to help at the store."

Josh turned to Roger. "What about you?"

"My parents flew to the Big Island today to see relatives. I'll ask when they get back tonight."

Josh nodded. "I'll ask my father if he was able to reach the helicopter pilot. Uh oh!"

"What?" Tank and Roger asked together.

Josh pointed through the open window that faced the outside walkway. "Look!"

All three boys rushed to the window and looked out. A barefoot man in a white aloha shirt* and matching pants was disappearing past the next apartment.

"It's Hotdog!" Tank exclaimed. He dropped his voice. "You think he was listening through the window?"

Josh nodded, again aware that there were no trades, so the air was totally still. "He sure was. That means he knows about the map."

Roger pursed his lips. "Yeah, he heard, but he didn't see the map. He can't get there without it."

Tank gently rubbed his sunburned nose. "But now that he knows about it, maybe he'll try to get a look at it."

Roger held up the map. "What'll we do with this?"

"Let's give it to my father," Josh suggested. "He won't let anything happen to it. Hotdog might try to take it from one of us, but not my dad."

The three friends agreed. Josh carefully folded the map and carried it down to the second floor, accompanied by Tank and Roger. Mr. Ladd promised to keep the map safely.

For the next two days, Josh fretted impatiently while his father completed arrangements for Mr. Slayton to fly them to the "lagoon." The boys and their families tried hard to keep Hotdog from knowing when the flight to Kauai was planned.

On the day of the trip, both Tank and Roger had to stay behind. Tank's father was still shorthanded in the stockroom of the department store he managed, and Roger's parents expected relatives, including two of Roger's cousins, on a return visit from the Big Island.

The trades were blowing, and the Honolulu sky was filled with puffy, white clouds as Mary Ladd dropped off her husband and son at the airport. As Josh and his father took their seats in the T-tailed short-haul jet for the quick flight to Kauai, Josh felt a rising excitement. He wondered, "Will we find the wreck? Will the guy with the sword be waiting?"

Josh barely noticed the Hawaiian music on the plane's public address system or the cabin's decorations of petroglyphs* and kihilis.* The stewardess, dressed in a bright-red- and yellow-flowered muumuu,* announced an estimated flying time of thirty-one minutes from Honolulu to Kauai's airport at Lihue.*

Father and son said little as the engines screamed toward full power. The plane hurtled down the runway and lifted into the air. A few seconds later, unseen by Josh or his father, a private jet lifted off from the same airport. The needle-nosed craft followed the interisland commercial jet into the clouds.

The aircraft banked as it climbed, and Josh could see the incredibly beautiful blue-green ocean below. It was so shallow that submerged land could be seen for quite a distance.

Josh's father, sitting next to the window, announced, "There's Pearl Harbor. I never realized how flat Ford Island is. Can you see, Son?"

Josh, restrained by his seat belt, stretched his neck. "It's like an airport runway."

"That's the battleship Arizona." John Ladd said the words softly. The ship, sunk by the Japanese, was clearly visible where it still rested near Ford Island. Mr. Ladd's voice took on a slight touch of the history teacher. "She was sunk when the Japanese pulled their sneak attack on the morning of December 7, 1941. More than a thousand American men went down with her. They're still entombed there."

Josh nodded, remembering his visit to the glistening white monument that straddled the Arizona. The memorial marked the spot where World War II had officially started for the United States.

The scene slid by and was soon replaced by neat fields of sugarcane. The plane bounced slightly from turbulence as it left clear skies and entered cumulus clouds.

"Dad?" Josh lowered his voice and looked around to be sure no one else could hear. "Do you suppose that plane we found could have helped sink the Arizona?"

"Who knows? I'm more interested in that Japanese man who chased you boys."

The jet banked slightly to the right. As the wing dipped, Josh glanced out the small cabin window. Far back, the sun reflected off a sleek private jet, like a black shadow in the sky. For a moment, Josh had an uneasy feeling the jet was following them. Then he shrugged. "Couldn't be!" he told himself.

Chapter Six

BACK INTO THE JUNGLE

Josh forced himself to forget about the private plane that might be following them. He turned to his father and said, "Is it possible that the pilot of that crashed plane could've stayed alive in the jungle all alone for half a century?"

"It's very unlikely, yet I remember when a Japanese soldier was found hiding out on a Pacific island about forty years after the war ended. He was quite a celebrity when he finally returned to Japan."

"He didn't know the war was over?"

"I forget the details, but I think that's right."

"Maybe this man I saw doesn't know the war's over, either."

"Maybe, but it could be something else, too. Remember all those television programs we saw some time back about Vietnam War veterans who 'dropped out' of society?"

"Oh, yeah. Some didn't want to return to normal life. So they still lived alone in the woods."

53

"I've known a few men in my life who got tired of things and became hermits or recluses. Maybe this fellow who chased you kids is one of those."

Josh shook his head. "I'm pretty sure he was Japanese, and he was old."

"Lots of Americans of Japanese descent live in Hawaii, Son. Maybe you saw one of them who just wants to live alone. Anyway, I still think he was just trying to scare you away."

"You really don't think he'll try to hurt us?"

"Of course not! I wouldn't have brought you along if I'd thought that. But it's too good a story possibility not to check it out."

"Hotdog'll be mad if it really turns out to be a good story and we beat him at getting it on video."

"Hotdog?"

"That's what us kids call Greg Grayson. You know, he's the television reporter who just moved into the apartments—the one who eavesdropped outside Roger's window when we were drawing the map."

John Ladd patted his shirt pocket. "Well, he didn't get the map."

"Do you think he'd try to follow us?"

"I doubt it."

Josh started to say he wasn't so sure, but his father pointed out the small window. "I can see land coming up. We're almost there."

Josh felt the cabin tilt slightly downward. They slid

through a small cloud that seemed like fog on the wings. Then the jet broke into full sun, and Josh glimpsed a point of land. Kauai was called "The Garden Isle" because it was very green. As the right wing swung sharply down, Josh saw a lighthouse. The plane skimmed over cane fields and landed with a hard bump.

As other passengers stood and moved into the aisles, Josh carefully pulled his video camera from under the seat in front of him. He said a silent prayer that he'd be able to find the wrecked plane again and get some good footage—without being attacked by the swordsman.

Josh and his dad joined other passengers on the ground. The boy saw acres of tall sugarcane stalks being bent by the warm trade winds. He also saw kiawe,* the thorny, shrublike trees that seemed to grow everywhere they weren't cut back.

Just then the small, black jet settled smoothly onto the runway. Josh watched it slowing down and wondered if it had really been following them.

His thoughts were interrupted by his father. "There's our pilot, Son." John Ladd waved with his free hand and began walking rapidly toward the tall, slender man approaching him.

"That's his helicopter over there," Josh replied. He hurried to keep up with his long-legged, fast-moving father, but the video camera slowed him down. He said, "You sure Mr. Slayton can find the blue lagoon and the tree where he picked us up?"

"He told me on the phone he's pretty sure we can find both places. The hard part's going to be finding the wreck after you and I enter the jungle."

The pilot came to meet them. He had a bald spot in the middle of his pale-blond hair. "Good to see you again, Mr. Ladd, Josh," he said with a warm smile. "This everything?" He indicated the video camera Josh carried and the leather case holding his father's still camera.

"No, we've got backpacks, canteens, compasses, and other equipment we had to check as baggage."

"We'll pick those up over there," the pilot said, indicating a baggage claim area to which other passengers from Honolulu were already heading. "Josh, you want me to help with that camera?"

"No, thanks. I'm used to it."

They reclaimed their equipment and stowed it aboard the helicopter, then climbed into the cabin. The pilot took the right front position, with Josh beside him. Mr. Ladd took the back seat.

As they buckled their belts, Josh's father said, "Thanks for arranging this charter, Mr. Slayton. If this goes the way my son and I expect, we'll have a special story. Maybe we can shoot some footage of you and your aircraft as part of the feature."

The pilot grinned and said, "I don't suppose *you* can tell me any details, either."

Josh spoke quickly. "No, I'm sorry."

His father asked a little sharply, "What do you mean,

'Any details, either?' "

"Oh, some television news guy from Honolulu's been calling to ask me to take him to the same place where I picked up your kids the other day."

Josh exclaimed, "He did?"

"Sure did. Must've called half a dozen times with different offers. Each time, he'd sweeten the deal a little."

"What'd you tell him?" Josh asked anxiously.

"He rubbed me wrong. Pushed too hard, I guess. So I told him no."

Josh and his father exchanged glances, then John Ladd turned back to the pilot. "Does anyone else know about these calls?"

"Why, sure! Everybody in the office knows. The guy made such a pest of himself that it was the talk of the office."

"Other pilots included?" Josh asked.

Mr. Slayton nodded. "Yep. But since he insisted on my flying him, we all figured it had something to do with the story Josh and his friends told about being chased by a World War II Japanese swordsman."

He reached for large headphones. "Put your headsets on. Soon's I finish talking to the tower, we'll be on our way and will have to talk to each other through an inter-com. Gets too noisy in here to talk otherwise."

Father and son adjusted their headsets while Josh thought about what the pilot had said. Even if Hotdog couldn't hire Mr. Slayton, other chopper pilots might be able to take him to the blue lagoon—maybe even to the lone tree by the gorge. Mr. Slayton must have discussed all those landmarks in his talks with other pilots at Princeville. Of course, without the map the boys had drawn, Hotdog probably couldn't really find the downed plane.

After the helicopter lifted from the pad and reached cruising altitude, heading northwest, the pilot switched to the intercom. Josh heard Mr. Slayton's voice in the earphones. "You two in a race to beat this television reporter to the site of that crashed plane?"

Father and son exchanged glances. Mr. Ladd admitted, "I suppose you could say that."

"Well, you'd better be successful pretty fast or it'll be too late for anybody."

Josh felt a stirring of alarm. "Why's that?"

"Rain's coming," the pilot answered. "The start of enough rain to cover a four- or five-story building."

The wettest spot on earth! Josh told himself, "We should have that footage and be out of here long before the downpour starts." Josh removed the video camera from the case to shoot the incredibly beautiful landscapes below.

The pilot's voice sounded in the boy's ears. "Don't lean the camera against the window. You'll get a fuzzy picture because the chopper bounces and jumps around sometimes."

"I remember," Josh said, bringing the camera to his

eye and focusing ahead of him.

Kauai had fantastic beaches tucked between soaring mountains and a beautiful, blue-green ocean. There were narrow, remote, hidden valleys of intense green. Countless waterfalls cascaded in silent splendor down hundreds of feet to splash into jewel-like lakes or meandering rivers.

There were also areas of startlingly barren, terracotta-colored cliffs. Above all, there was the massive, dead volcano that had created the island. Its peak was wrapped in protective clouds.

"We're almost there," Clay Slayton said into his passengers' earphones. The helicopter banked sharply to the right, making Josh's stomach lurch toward his mouth. But he concentrated on holding the camera steady and exposing the tape.

"There's the little lake where we landed the other day," the pilot said. "We'll come back and land there after we fly over the jungle to that banyan tree by the gorge."

Josh saw the blue lagoon slide by below. The open landing area fell behind.

"Here comes the rain forest," Mr. Slayton said. "Hold your camera steady, and I'll give you a good view over the landmarks you asked about."

Josh's father said, "I'll get out the map you boys drew so we can identify them."

Josh pointed to the fringe of jungle. "There's the lava shaft I told you about, Dad! See?"

"You're right, Son. It looks like the spear point of some huge giant. Must be five hundred feet high."

"That's where we entered the jungle." Josh spun in his seat. "Let's see the map from the air, Dad! Once we locate all the landmarks up here, we'll have a much better idea of where to look in the jungle."

Father and son examined the map while the pilot swooped low over the rain forest. It was so pretty from the air, but underneath the canopy of trees, Josh knew there was a giant, green prison that held strange secrets.

Josh strained for a glimpse of the jungle floor, but the canopy was too dense. He also tried unsuccessfully to locate some sign of the plane.

"Now," the pilot announced, "we'll head over to the place I picked up you boys." The chopper swooped over the rain forest toward an open spot. In a few seconds, Mr. Slayton added, "There it is!"

"I see it!" Josh's voice rose in excitement. "See, Dad? There's the lone banyan with the vines we used to swing across! See how deep that gorge is? And the little pond of water at the foot of the V the cliffs make?"

"I see it, Son."

The pilot banked the chopper. "Since there aren't any falls, that water in the little lake must seep through the ground and collect there."

"Is that possible?" Josh asked.

"Sure! This whole island is volcanic, you know. It's filled with lava tubes, some so big you can walk through them. And some of them can carry water like a giant pipe."

Josh knew the tubes had formed when the outside of the fresh magma, or lava, cooled faster than the inside. The inside lava finally flowed out, leaving a tube.

The chopper leveled off and headed back over a barren, rust-colored area toward the landing site. Soon Josh pointed. "There's the blue lagoon, Dad! We landed right over there in that little meadow to have our picnic!"

Mr. Slayton announced, "We'll land in exactly the same place, Josh."

As the pilot began to unload their gear, father and son climbed out of the helicopter. But as Mr. Ladd stepped down, his foot slipped, and he dropped the still camera from his hand. It cracked top down against a rock and bounced to the ground. "Oh, no!" he groaned.

Looking on, Josh said, "Is it all right, Dad?"

"I'll tell you in a second," he replied. Taking the camera out of its case, he raised the viewfinder to his eye and looked through. Then he tried to take a picture. "Aargh! The shutter's jammed. This camera is worthless until it comes back from a repair shop."

"Well, at least we have my video camera, Dad."

"It looks as though we're going to have to depend entirely on that, Son. There's no point in taking this one any farther."

"Excuse me," Mr. Slayton interrupted. "Sorry about your camera, but I've got a question. It's obvious you two aren't just looking for the downed Japanese aircraft the boys found, so are you really looking for The Phantom?"

He waited a moment, but when neither of the Ladds answered, he spoke again. "As I told you right after picking up the kids the other day, there've been rumors of a phantom up there on that mountain for decades."

"Who do you think it is?" Josh asked. He felt he could trust the pilot. After all, even if the man talked to Hotdog, the landmarks without the map wouldn't be enough to locate the plane.

Mr. Slayton replied, "Beats me. But I sure don't think it's a ghost, if that's what you mean."

Josh asked, "Do you suppose it could really be a Japanese pilot whose plane crashed after attacking Pearl Harbor?"

"It's a wild possibility, but if it is, he may not know the war is over. Watch out that he doesn't attack you."

He turned to Mr. Ladd. "I'm not sure about Josh, because he's so young. But you're a man, Mr. Ladd, so if that's a real warrior out there, he'd probably figure you're the enemy, and he might—"

Mr. Ladd interrupted. "I'm sure we'll be fine!"

Josh shivered, glancing at his father with sudden fear.

His father said, "Well, we're ready. Mr. Slayton, if we're not back by dark, notify the authorities." Then he produced a big roll of very thin monofilament fishing line. "We'll leave a trail so we can find our way back—or someone can follow us if we don't come back."

Father and son squared their backpacks, adjusted their canteens, and headed for the giant lava spear. They had barely entered the humid rain forest when Josh stopped suddenly. "Listen!" he whispered.

"What did you hear, Son?"

Josh's heart was beating too loudly for him to answer.

Chapter Seven

A SEARCH IN THE RAIN FOREST

Josh's father repeated, "What do you hear?"

The boy swiveled and looked back across the open area. "Another helicopter!" He tilted his face to the sky and scanned it quickly. "There!" He pointed. "It's coming in for a landing. That's got to be Hotdog!"

John Ladd shielded his eyes with his right hand and studied the approaching aircraft. "You're probably right. That poses a problem." He glanced down at the roll of monofilament fishing line. "If we unroll this as we go, that fellow can follow us."

"And if we don't, we might not be able to get back!" Josh dropped his eyes from the second helicopter to his father. "What'll we do?"

"Since this fishing line is almost invisible, Grayson may not see it. Besides, we've come too far to quit without trying. Let's go find that plane."

The father tied one end of the strong, almost-transparent line to the support root of a small banyan tree and began walking through the forest. The line played out from the spool, leaving a barely visible trail. "Which way, Son?"

"That way." He started veering to his right.

"Just a minute, Son." The boy turned around to see his father bending over a small, pretty plant. "You know what this is, Son?"

Josh was anxious to be far away from Hotdog or whoever was in the other helicopter. "No," Josh replied without slowing. They had gone only a few steps into the rain forest, but already it had swallowed them up. There was no sign or sound of the second helicopter.

"It's a sundew!" There was surprise in the man's voice. "It's a carnivorous plant! A flycatcher!"

Josh glanced at the tiny plant with its bell-shaped flowers. He had never seen an insect-eating plant before, but he didn't care just now. "Dad, we haven't got time to stop and look at things like that!" The boy's voice was sharper than he intended. To soften the impression, he added more gently, "Please! Let's hurry in case Hotdog's trying to follow us."

They moved deeper into the jungle for several minutes. Suddenly Josh froze, his body tense. His eyes probed the deep shadows ahead.

"What do you see, Son?"

"Just a movement, like an animal," Josh whispered. "Can't see it clearly yet. Mongoose, maybe."

"Can't be. Kauai never imported them to control cane rats as all the other islands did. Maybe a wild dog?"

The animal moved, slinking into the open. "It *is* a dog!" Josh said with relief. He had seen few domestic dogs since moving to Hawaii. Those he had seen were all very skinny, but this one was even worse. It was so thin that Josh thought if there were any sunshine, it would show right through the animal. It vanished into the underbrush with a low, frightened "Woof!"

Father and son moved on slowly, their eyes roaming the jungle. Josh went ahead, his dad playing out the fishing line to the end of the first spool. He motioned for Josh to stop while he took out a second roll and tied the two ends together. Then he continued unrolling as they pushed through the rain forest.

Josh was alert, trying to recognize landmarks, but the jungle all looked the same. He listened, every nerve strained, for the mysterious swordsman. Josh's eyes flickered across the underbrush, lifted to the trees, and continued on up to the thick canopy high overhead. He turned to check their back trail.

"Scared, Son?"

Josh swallowed hard before shaking his head. "Just edgy. I was thinking Hotdog might be following while that phantom or whoever he is waits up ahead."

The boy pressed on, pushing vines and leaves aside with one hand while cradling the video camera in the other. He recognized the myna birds' calls, remembering they usually were fairly quiet except at morning and evening. He also caught glimpses of many small birds he couldn't identify.

Josh began to get discouraged. Nothing really looked familiar. He couldn't find the wild animal trail that he, Tank, and Roger had been on when they discovered the plane.

The humidity was terrible, too. Josh reached into his shirt pocket to produce a pen and piece of paper on which he could make notes. The previous entry had been soaked through with his perspiration and was so blurry the words were indecipherable. "Yuck!" he said, replacing the damp paper. "The humidity is one thing I don't like about Hawaii, especially in this rain forest."

"How about taking a break, Son?" his dad said. "I could use some water."

They sat on a wide stump with wild ginger growing nearby. Each released a canteen from his belt and drank. Josh felt the cool water trickle down his throat. He wished he could finish the whole canteen, but he forced himself to stop and recap the container.

"Dad, do you think Hotdog's following us?"

"Your guess is as good as mine. But it won't do him any good unless we find that wreck. If we do, we'll have to get your camera working fast and then get back before he can find the plane, too."

"How long's it been?"

John Ladd glanced at his watch. "Little over an hour."

They got up and checked the trail behind them for sight or sound of someone following. There was none. They pushed on into the jungle.

Suddenly, a bird's alarm call sounded ahead. Josh turned and whispered to his father, "We're too far away for that bird to be warning about us."

Mr. Ladd listened, turning slowly, his eyes skimming brush and trees. "You're right. The bird's seen something or someone up ahead."

"Do—do you think whoever chased us boys—might be watching?"

"Could be. Go on quietly, and keep your eyes open!"

Suddenly, something moved in the dense underbrush off to their right. Father and son saw it at the same time. Their eyes focused on the spot, waiting for it to move again.

Josh's mind raced with possibilities. Another wild dog? A deer?

Josh heard a grunt, and his heart leaped into his mouth. He whispered hoarsely, "Dad, it's a wild hog!"

"Hold still! Those boars can be vicious!"

The animal wasn't big by domestic hog standards, but he was big enough. He stepped out into the open, tiny eyes focused on them. Great, white tusks curled out from his mouth, showing what terrible damage he could do to a man's legs. And if the man fell. . . .

"Don't move, Son!"

Josh had been thinking about running, although he had remained frozen like a statue since glimpsing the ugly, black brute. The animal grunted once, the end of its flat nose working as it sniffed the air. Would it run or attack?

A sharp crack sounded from the way Josh and his father had come. They turned in that direction. So did the boar. Josh stared into the jungle until tiny flecks of white light seemed to dance before his eyes. He blinked and turned to look at the hog.

It was gone.

Josh glanced fearfully around, half expecting to see the animal within a few feet of his vulnerable legs. His father spoke quietly. "You wouldn't think such a big beast could move so silently."

Josh nodded. He would have expected the wild boar to crash through the underbrush like a boulder rolling downhill.

He heard his father's relieved sigh. "Well, whatever made that cracking sound scared off our hairy hog, for which I'm grateful. But I've been thinking: maybe we'd better turn back."

Josh had been thinking the same thing, but the idea of going back without any success at all bothered him. "But we're getting closer to the plane!" he protested.

"What if there are other wild hogs around? They might not run off the way this one did. I think we'd better go back."

Reluctantly, Josh started to obey. Then he stopped, pointed, and said, "Hey! I think that tree looks familiar! Let's take a look!"

"Well, okay, but if you're wrong, we head for the—oops!"

Startled at the exclamation, Josh spun around to see the fishing line jerking against his father's hands. "Looks like you've got a bite, Dad!" Josh joked.

"It's not a fish. You can be sure of that. Something ran into it back there in the undergrowth."

"Wild boar?"

"Could be. Well, what about that tree? Is it your landmark?"

"I'm pretty sure it is. If I remember right, the trail is just—yes! There it is! So the plane isn't far—" He had started to turn around to face his father but abruptly broke off his thought. He tensed, looking back the way they'd come. "Look!" he whispered.

Something was moving through the rain forest. At first, Josh saw only a shadow. Then slowly he made out a human form. Maybe it hadn't been an animal that made the fishing line jerk! He leaned forward, gripping the video camera, trying to pick out some details of the moving shadow that was part of deeper shadows.

"What do you think, Dad?" the boy whispered.

"Can't tell much, except he's being very cautious. Quick! Get down behind something and hold still!"

Josh started to obey, then asked, "What if it's the old man with the sword?"

"Shh! Get down!"

Silently, Josh obeyed. He sank out of sight behind the

huge, exposed root of a banyan tree. Holding his breath and clutching the video camera, he drew his legs under him so he could jump and run if necessary. Then he waited as the shadowy figure slipped noiselessly toward them.

Chapter Eight

JUNGLE SURPRISES

Josh took a slow, deep breath to try quieting his speeding heart. Whoever was moving through the rain forest was being very careful. He moved slowly and silently, a barely visible figure in the deep shadows. Josh raised his head slightly above the banyan tree root for a clearer look.

"Maybe he'll go right on by," Josh told himself hopefully. "But he's walking funny. Oh! I see why! He's following the fishing line! He must've bumped into it. Otherwise, he probably wouldn't ever have seen it. But he's not touching it now."

The boy wanted to relay that information to his father, who crouched behind a ti plant a few feet closer to the approaching figure. Then Josh noticed that his father still held the spool of monofilament line in his hand. "Oh, no!" Josh thought. "That guy'll follow the line right to Dad!"

What to do? If Josh tried to whisper a warning, it might be heard by the approaching stranger.

His heart sped up again as he tried to decide what to do. Then he noticed a single shaft of sunlight slanting down from the tree canopy to the forest floor. "He'll walk into that in a second, and I can see who he is! And I can get his picture!"

Josh barely breathed as he eased the video camera to his right eye. He tensed, finger touching the red "on" button, waiting. The shadowy figure moved closer and closer to the sunbeam. "One more step," Josh told himself.

The person was momentarily spotlighted in the sun's ray. Josh sucked in his breath in surprise. "It's just an old Oriental man!"

Josh's right forefinger pressed to start the camera. A red light winked on in the lower center of the viewfinder, and a low hum indicated the video tape was rolling. The sensitive black microphone above the lens automatically recorded sound at the same time.

The boy studied the man through the viewfinder. His hair was long and uncut, but definitely gray. The face was lined with wrinkles. He hadn't shaved in a long time, yet his gray facial hair was sparse and thin. It wasn't really much of a beard.

He wore only a pair of ancient cutoff jeans and the two-toed slippers favored by many Hawaiians of Japanese ancestry. From a string belt around his waist hung an old knife scabbard about a foot long.

"Probably a hermit," Josh told himself as the stranger

moved out of the sunbeam and into the steamy jungle shadows again. The boy shifted the camera to follow, knowing all adjustments for light and distance would be made automatically.

"Or—" Josh's thoughts jumped, but he kept exposing the video tape. "Or maybe it's The Phantom who chased Tank and Roger and me. No, this guy doesn't have the same clothes or a sword."

The urge to whisper to his father was strong, but Josh forced himself to be quiet. The old man eased cautiously closer, his eyes on the fishing line that rested on the jungle's undergrowth. In another few seconds, he would see that the line led down to Mr. Ladd's hands.

Suddenly, the man stopped dead still. He looked toward the deep shadows where the Ladds crouched. "He's seen us!" Josh thought. He kept the video tape rolling. It wouldn't stop until Josh pushed the red button again.

The stranger held his position for a second. Then he pivoted on silent feet and slipped into the deeper underbrush. Josh raised himself enough to follow the man's movements with the camera. Suddenly, he vanished.

Josh stopped the camera and stood up. "Now how in the world did he do that?"

Josh wasn't aware he'd whispered aloud until his father also stood and answered, "Let's go find out."

"Careful! He's got a knife!"

"He's also a very old man and didn't look dangerous to me, Son."

Mr. Ladd laid his spool of line on the ground and led the way to the spot where the man had disappeared. Josh followed, not knowing whether he was just excited or scared about what they'd find.

His father stopped and pointed. "There's your answer," he said in a stage whisper. "A giant lava tube. He went through it."

Josh tried to see inside, but it was too dark to see more than a foot or so into the black, volcanic tunnel.

His father said softly, "Get your camera ready. I'm going to take a peek inside."

"Careful, Dad!" Josh raised the camera to his eye and began shooting as his father slowly approached the tube's entrance, bent, and peered inside.

Josh was still taking footage when his father turned and shrugged. "Can't see a thing, Son. We'll get a flashlight and come back."

Josh turned the camera off again and lowered it from his shoulder. "Okay, but first let's see if we can find that plane."

His father hesitated. "Are you sure it's close?"

"I'm pretty sure the trail's right on the other side of that tree. If it is, the plane's not much farther."

"Okay, Son. If we find a trail there, we'll go on and try to find the wreckage. But if there's no trail, we go back to our helicopter and try another day."

Josh was a little concerned about the mysterious man's possibly reappearing, but he was more anxious to shoot the plane wreckage. He was relieved, then, when he found the trail. "See?" he turned triumphantly to face his father. "That's it! The plane's got to be just off the trail a little farther on."

Josh rushed ahead, feeling the spongy jungle floor beneath his feet. His eyes skittered ahead and off to the side, watching for sight of the crashed plane. It would be easier to find this time because the boys had removed some of the vines and leaves from the crumpled mass.

"There!" Josh stopped and pointed. "Just like I told you!" He was tempted to run forward and re-examine the downed aircraft, but he remembered his primary purpose in coming. He shifted the camera to his shoulder. "Dad, I'd better get my shots right away. You walk up to the wreck so there'll be some action. Okay?"

"You're going to make me a movie star, are you, Son?" John Ladd joked. He dropped the spool of line in the trail and pushed into the brush. Josh started shooting as his father approached the fuselage. "You're right, Josh! It is a Japanese plane! World War II type!"

"I'll zoom in while you pull some vines and things off," Josh said. "Point to the red emblem or something."

When his father obeyed, Josh stopped the camera. "Now walk around the rest of the plane to the cockpit and look in."

"Wouldn't you rather I shot some tape so you could be in the next scenes?" his dad said.

"Well, yeah! Thanks, Dad!"

They changed places. Josh handed the camera to his father and walked back to the fuselage. It was such an exciting experience that Josh wanted to shout with joy, but there was something sad about the wrecked aircraft, so he remained outwardly subdued. He remembered the camera's microphone and tried to describe what he saw as he slowly uncovered more of the fuselage.

Finally his father suggested, "We'd better get back. You've surely got enough tape to interest the television stations and cable networks."

Josh nodded and walked toward his father. "Do you think they'll pay enough so I can bring Grandma over?"

"I'm sure of it, Son."

Josh retrieved the camera and looked down at the spool on the trail. "What'll we do with the fishing line?"

"I could roll it back up as we go, but I think we'll just leave it here. The old Asian has already found it. But nobody else'll come this way until we come back with a flashlight to look into that tube."

"How about Hotdog?"

"That's a good question. We don't want him to find it. Oh, I know! I'll rewind part of the line and then just leave it somewhere back the way we came. From there we can find our way back here when we come with a light."

"Who do you think the old Oriental was?"

"He's probably some recluse. I'll rewind the line until we get past the tube where he disappeared."

Josh studied the jungle around them. "What if he removes it?"

"Then we'll have to find our way back here the same way we did this time. Come on. Let's go."

Mr. Ladd rolled the fishing line back onto the spool. Josh walked close behind, glancing everywhere to see if the old man would reappear. He didn't. Josh wasn't easily scared, but there was something spooky about this place.

"Guess this is far enough," John Ladd said finally. He set the spool down under an exposed tree root where it wouldn't be seen easily. "Now let's get back to the chopper."

They moved quickly, their eyes following the almost-invisible line that showed the way they'd come. Josh was so excited he bubbled with speculation over what the cable and television news people would say about the tape.

"Banzai!"

The sudden shout behind Josh almost made him drop the camera. He spun in sudden terror, expecting to see a sword being swung at him.

"Look out, Son!"

Josh glimpsed someone fairly explode from the dense undergrowth toward him. He caught a flash of high altitude flying clothes and bright yellow boots. Instantly, the strange figure was upon him. Two arms reached out and seized the camera.

"Hey!" Josh cried, trying to hang on.

The camera was violently jerked from his hands. The

figure uttered a triumphant cry and leaped back into the underbrush. The whole incident had lasted only a few seconds.

"Dad! He's got the camera!" Josh started to follow the sounds of flight into the brush, but his father's sharp command stopped him.

"No, Josh! Don't go after him!"

"But Dad, he doesn't have the sword!"

"We'd get lost trying to follow him! Let's get out of here!"

"But my camera!"

"Joshua! Let's go! Now!"

Josh ran the few steps to his father. "Dad, without that tape, I can't bring Grandma over here!"

"Can't help that! Now come on, please!"

Josh let out an unhappy sigh and followed his father. "Can we get another camera before we come back?"

"We'll see, Son. Right now I want to get out of here and think this thing through!"

They followed the line back to the jungle's edge. As they stepped into the open, Josh saw two helicopters.

"Dad, I was right! Hotdog followed us!"

Clay Slayton, their pilot, greeted them with two quick questions. "Where's your camera? And didn't you see that television newsman?"

Mr. Ladd answered, "So he did follow us?"

"Landed in that other chopper right after you two entered the rain forest."

"Was he alone?" Josh interrupted, turning to look at the green prison.

"No. He had a television cameraman and a sound man with him. They were loaded down with equipment. But if you didn't see them, maybe they're lost. Their pilot's taking a nap in the cabin. Think we should notify the authorities to search for those three?"

Josh didn't like Hotdog, but he was still a human being. He also had two other men with him. Josh remembered how the thought of being lost in the jungle had bothered him. He asked uncertainly, "Should we look for them, Dad?"

"That's not practical. We'd probably get lost, too. No, we'd better do as Mr. Slayton suggested. Let a trained search and rescue team handle this."

"What if they run into the guy who grabbed my camera? Or even the old Oriental man?"

The pilot asked quickly, "Who grabbed your camera?"

"The same guy in the old flying clothes and yellow boots that Tank, Roger, and I saw before."

"You're kidding." Mr. Slayton's surprise was real.

"No," Josh assured him. "And there was another old man in there. He vanished into a big lava tube."

Mr. Slayton cocked his head suspiciously and looked from father to son, then seemed satisfied. "You're not fooling me? That's really what happened? There is a phantom in there?"

"That's really what happened," Mr. Ladd said. "I think

it was a man, although he certainly disappeared as a phantom might. Anyway, let's go."

The pilot led the way back to the aircraft, saying he'd notify the tower and they could alert search authorities. At the chopper, Mr. Slayton asked, "So there are two old men in that jungle? What do you make of it?"

Mr. Ladd replied, "I don't know yet."

Josh asked anxiously, "We'll come back, won't we, Dad?"

His father pulled himself into the cabin and spoke over his shoulder. "That remains to be seen, Son."

"I've got to get my camera back—and my video tape! Everything depends on it!"

"We'll talk everything through on the flight back, Josh. Now get in and buckle up. There's something mighty strange going on, and I'm not sure what to do about it."

The pilot buckled his seat belt and settled the big ear-phones on his head. "Wonder what the phantom's going to do with your camera, Josh?"

"I don't know, but I'm not going to let him keep it!" He turned to his father and asked, "Are we?"

"We'll see, Son. We'll see!"

"We can't let Hotdog beat us!"

"He may have already, Son. He's still in there and might stumble on the plane the same way you did."

Josh felt sick as the helicopter lifted off and headed for Lihue. Questions popped into his head, and each made him a little more unwell.

Was there really a phantom? Or was it fear of the unknown that made people think there was? Who was the old Oriental who'd disappeared into the lava tube? Did Hotdog find the wrecked plane? Was he going to beat Josh in getting footage to the news services and ruin his plans? Could Josh come back with another camera and solve the mystery of the blue lagoon before it was too late?

A bunch of little fears began nibbling at the edges of Josh's mind, and more were sure to come.

Chapter Nine

A WARNING

While Josh's mother and sister were preparing dinner that night, Josh and his little brother stood on their apartment lanai. Down below, in the parking lot, neighborhood kids played with skateboards. Josh was only vaguely aware of their presence.

Nathan asked, "You worried about Hotdog?"

Josh nodded, leaning his elbows on the flat, wooden rail. "Yes, but I don't know why I should be. He brags a lot and only cares about himself."

"You know what he told me yesterday?"

Josh shook his head, watching the moon rise above Diamond Head.

"He said, 'I'll do anything to get a story, and that means I'm not going to let your big brother beat me to that plane wreck! No kid's going to beat me, so he'd better stay out of my way!'"

Josh felt anger stir within. Hotdog wanted to be first just because that's the way he was. Josh wanted to be first with the tapes so he could bring his grandmother over from the Mainland. He didn't want his father risking their newspaper and maybe having to move the family back to California. It just wasn't fair!

Nathan broke Josh's train of thought. "You think Hotdog's really lost in the jungle with those other TV guys?"

"Maybe not. There wasn't anything on the local news about it. That probably means they're okay."

"You're right! Look!" Nathan pointed down the narrow street that led to the parking lot.

"That's his car," Josh said.

The fire-engine-red sports car whirled up the street with the roar of a powerful engine. The playing kids jumped aside while Hotdog whipped the car into his carport and got out. His clothes were dirty and torn. His hands and face were scratched, and he didn't look happy when he saw Josh.

"Okay, Kid," the man growled, "you win this one. But there's no way a punk like you is going to beat me! You got me lost!"

Josh wanted to say, "It's not my fault!" but he kept his mouth shut. Hotdog wouldn't listen to reason anyway.

"Dinner!" Tiffany called from inside the apartment. "Then upstairs to the Okamotos' for dessert!"

Josh knew the visit was to discuss going back to Kauai. He turned away from the lanai rail with a sigh, glad Hotdog was all right but knowing there were more problems ahead with him.

After dinner, the Ladds and Catletts climbed to the third-story Okamoto apartment. Everyone removed shoes at the door and entered barefoot or in stocking feet. "Time for learning Japanese again," Mrs. Okamoto said with a smile.

Josh's parents liked the idea of learning about other cultures. Josh, Tiffany, and Nathan were encouraged to do the same. Mrs. Ladd replied to their hosts, "*Goshotai arigato*," which Josh remembered meant, "Thank you for inviting me."

"Hai!"* Josh added.

"Dozo,"* Mrs. Okamoto said, indicating a large monkeypod* coffee table that glistened with a high gloss. Everyone sat on the floor, Japanese style. The women and girls kneeled, their knees forward so they sat on their legs with their shoeless feet sticking out behind them. The position was uncomfortable for those unused to it.

The men and boys sat with legs crossed in what Josh had always considered "Indian style." It wasn't so bad for Josh, Tank, and Roger, but Mr. Ladd and Mr. Catlett were soon squirming and changing positions.

Learning something about Japanese customs was made easier because Roger's maternal grandmother was Tokyo-born. She had sometimes joined the Ladds and Catletts in the Okamoto apartment. Mrs. Yamaguchi had insisted on talking to her grandson in her native tongue and encouraged him to answer in the same. Roger had resisted, however, being content with knowing Pidgin and regular English.

The Okamoto apartment was decorated with the Kabuki dolls Roger's grandmother had made. There were hand-somely robed samurai* warriors and women clothed in beautiful kimonos,* their faces painted white as flour. Japanese motifs weren't uncommon in Hawaii. Even haoles who had served in the military in Japan often had Japanese themes in their homes.

John Ladd brought up the reason for the gathering. "You've all heard about the mystery on Kauai, so you've had time to come to some conclusions. Who wants to speak first?"

For a moment, no one spoke. Josh let his eyes roam around the living room, afraid the adults would suggest they give up trying to solve the mystery and get his camera back.

Tank's father finally cleared his throat. "Well," he began, then paused. He looked at his son and daughter sitting across the low table. Josh waited anxiously for the slender, wiry man to continue. Sam Catlett's blond hair was always perfectly styled. He usually wore the finest tropical-weight suits from the department store he managed in Honolulu. Tonight he had on light-weight gray slacks and a white shirt patterned after a Filipino wedding shirt.

"From a practical viewpoint," Sam Catlett continued, "I think it's too risky for the boys and one man to go back into that jungle. What's a video camera compared to possibly having someone hurt or injured—especially with the so-called Phantom there?"

His pretty wife, Barbara, shifted her weight and wiggled her bare toes behind her. "Sam's right," she said. "It's too risky. I don't want Tank to go back."

Josh wanted to protest, "But that tape's got pictures of the wrecked plane and the old Oriental man! I was going to sell the video and use the money to bring my grandma over here!" Instead he suggested, "We could all go: Mr. Catlett, Dad, Mr. Okamoto, and us three boys. We'd be safe with so many of us."

Nobody said anything. Josh's father looked at his wife and said, "Mary?"

"You all know how I feel. I think you've already taken too many chances."

Josh groaned inwardly. Three strikes! But this wasn't a ball game. Roger's parents hadn't spoken, and neither had Josh's father. There was still a chance.

John Ladd rocked sideways to ease the discomfort in his crossed-leg position. "Mr. Okamoto?" he said, nodding toward him.

Roger's father was a stocky, strongly built man with traces of gray in his black hair. He had a wide, friendly smile and an easy manner that made everyone like him. He sat with his back straight, wearing a blue-green aloha shirt outside his matching casual pants.

"I would not like to go against such lovely ladies," he said, "but boys will be boys, as the old saying goes. If

I were Josh, I would want my camera back. Most of all, I would want to know the answers to all the questions that have been raised by these recent events."

Josh wanted to stand up and cheer, but he simply exchanged a smile with Tank and Roger and waited.

Mr. Ladd said, "Mrs. Okamoto?"

She was shorter, more slender, with closely cropped black hair that barely touched her shoulders. "At the risk of offending my guests and new haole friends," she said with a smile, "I stand with my husband."

Josh nodded. Two for; three against, with his father's opinion yet to be given. Josh had been staring at a pale, ivory-colored shoji screen decorated with long-tailed birds of blue and red. Now his eyes snapped to his father.

"I'm afraid we're equally divided," he said. "I favor Josh's being allowed to try recovering his camera."

In spite of his determination to be quiet, Josh burst out, "But a tie's no good!"

Tank muttered, "That's right!"

His older sister whispered, "Shh!"

"Don't shush me, Marsha!" Tank hissed under his breath.

Josh lightly punched his friend in the ribs. "Not now!" he said.

Tiffany asked, "Dad, how're you going to decide?"

John Ladd looked slowly around the room. "We need an outside, neutral opinion."

"Like whose?" his wife asked.

"How about Dr. Chin?"

Josh's eyes darted around all six adults. He saw the Catletts exchange glances and nod. So did Josh's mother. That left Roger's parents. They were Buddhists,* so how would they react to the counsel of the Chinese pastor of the church where the Catletts and Ladds worshiped?

Roger's father said, "I have confidence in Dr. Chin's wisdom."

His wife nodded. "Me, too."

"Good!" Josh's father said. "I'll call him and see if we can set up an appointment. Whatever he says, we'll do. Agreed?"

Josh was delighted to see all the parents nod.

Mrs. Okamoto stood effortlessly from her kneeling position while the other two mothers rolled off their knees and rose slowly. Roger's mother announced, "For dessert, I have Japanese tempura-fried bananas with green tea ice cream."

All the kids except Josh let out joyful yells. There was something special about the hot and cold dish. It was made of locally grown bananas dipped in tempura batter and fried, then served with a very creamy, pistachio-green ice cream that tasted faintly of tea.

But for perhaps the first time in his life, Josh didn't care about dessert. He struggled to his feet, nearly falling over in his effort. He grinned at Tank and Roger and said, "Hey! We've still got a chance!"

"A chance for what?" Tank muttered. "To get your

camera back and solve the mystery, or to get caught by that wild man with the sword?"

At first Josh was annoyed at his friend, but then he saw Tank grin. "Let's find out whether we get to go or not," Josh said, returning the grin. "But I sure hope we can go before Hotdog gets there!"

Josh also thought of the fast-approaching deadline for his father to find out about the bank loan. "I'm running in two races at once," he told himself, "so I've got to get my footage first. But what if Dr. Chin doesn't think it's safe to go back to the jungle?"

The next evening, Josh was in his room writing a letter to Grandma Ladd when he heard a knock at the apartment door. Then he heard his mother cross from the kitchen where she and Tiffany were removing plates and glasses from the dishwasher. "Oh, Dr. Chin!" Mary Ladd's voice came down the hallway to Josh's ears. "Please come in."

Josh dropped his pen, jumped up, and hurried toward the living room. He heard his mother protest, "Oh, you don't have to take your shoes off, Pastor!"

"Sorry to disagree, Mrs. Ladd," Dr. Chin replied, "but you take your shoes off when you come to my house. It is only right that I take mine off in yours."

Josh crossed the living room to greet the slight man with salt-and-pepper hair. It was cut short and combed from the ears back to the center so it seemed to form a ridge in the middle of his forehead. Josh had never understood why the otherwise neatly dressed man wore his hair in such a manner. "Hi, Dr. Chin!" Josh said.

"Ah, Joshua! How nice to see you again!" The pastor extended his hand and peered over the top of his bifocals. "Your father told me about your exciting adventures on Kauai. Are you all right?"

"I'm fine. Dad had to run Nathan over to his Sunday school teacher's house. They're having a class party. Dad'll be right back."

Mrs. Ladd gestured toward an occasional chair by the louvered window. "Please come in and sit down. I'll tell my daughter you're here. We're all eager to get your opinion."

The pastor finished removing his plain, black dress shoes. "Ah, yes! Your husband told me some of the details on the phone. Perhaps Joshua will fill me in on everything while we wait for Mr. Ladd to return?" He stepped into the room and crossed in black-stockinged feet to the chair while Mrs. Ladd went back to the kitchen to help Tiffany finish emptying the dishwasher.

Josh plopped down on the white rug and leaned against the side of the television cabinet. "Dr. Chin, you don't know how much it'll mean for you to see my side of this— mine and Tank's and Roger's, I mean."

"Then I shall pray for the wisdom of Solomon, Joshua," he said.

There was another knock at the door. Josh looked up and saw Manuel Souza through the sliding screen door. "Hi, Manuel," Josh said. "I can't come out right now.

Our pastor's here."

"I've got to talk to you, Josh!" Manuel insisted.

"Not now!"

"Right now!" Manuel made impatient beckoning movements with his hands. "Meet me by the be-still tree."

"Well, I—"

"Hurry!" Manuel called through the screen door. He turned and hustled down the outside concrete stairs.

Josh made his apology to Dr. Chin, slipped on his zoris, and slap-slapped down the stairs and across the parking lot. There were outside lights, but Josh had a hard time seeing Manuel until he moved out of the dense shadows of the be-still tree.

"Manuel," he said, "what's so important?"

Manuel lowered his voice confidentially. "Just a couple of minutes ago, Kong came to my house with a message for you."

Josh was suddenly interested. "What'd he say? And why did he give the message to you?"

"He didn't want to wait until he could catch you away from your parents, and he knew you'd come out to talk to me. As for the message, he told me Hotdog had promised to make him famous—get him on a TV newscast or something—if he could get you to take him— Hotdog—to the plane crash."

"He what?"

"And if you don't do it, Kong told me, he'll make life miserable for you. Tank and Roger, too."

Josh moaned. "Oh, no!"

Manuel's head bobbed vigorously in the semidarkness. "Oh, yes! And he said he'd be after you this fall in school, too, not just the rest of this summer vacation."

"Oh, Manuel!"

"Kong also said if I didn't tell you right away, he'd punch me out!"

Josh nodded slowly, a sick feeling inside. "Well, you're off the hook. I just wish I were." He started to walk back toward the apartment.

Manuel raised his voice but still kept it at a hoarse whisper. "There's one thing more."

Josh stopped and looked at Manuel.

"Kong says you've got to take Hotdog to the plane before the weekend, or you're going to wish you had!"

Chapter Ten

A CHOICE OF DANGERS

Josh climbed the apartment stairs with an awful feeling in his stomach. He thought, "Everything's gone wrong! The Phantom stole my video camera with the cassette I was planning to sell. That means there's no money to bring Grandma over unless Dad borrows it.

"If he does that, he'll have to put up the newspaper as collateral. Since it's still losing money, he might not be able to repay the loan. Then he'd lose the paper, and that would break his heart.

"If he loses the paper, we might also have to move back to the Mainland, because it's cheaper to live there. But then I'd be separated from Tank, and I don't ever want that to happen again! Time's running out, too!

"Now Kong says that if I don't lead Hotdog to that wrecked plane, he'll make my life miserable all through the school year!" Josh paused outside the apartment and absently kicked off his zoris. "What should I do?" he asked himself. "If I tell Dad or Mom what Kong said, they might not believe he'd really do anything."

Kong was a bully who picked on anyone he thought he could dominate. It didn't matter if the victim was a haole or a local, although Kong especially disliked malihinis. "Unless I do what he said, I'll be his main victim!" Josh thought.

Tank had been Kong's principal victim last year. Tank had already warned Josh that Kong would probably include both boys in his daily activities next year. It'd be even worse if Josh failed to heed Kong's threat.

"But if I give in to him," Josh muttered aloud, "Hotdog will get the video tape, and I'll get nothing. There'll be no way I can bring Grandma over. But I don't want to have to face getting punched out all year, either. So maybe I'd better do what Kong says. But what if Dad won't let me go with Hotdog?"

His father said from inside, "What'd you say, Son?"

"What?" Josh asked, blinking and moving into the apartment. "Oh, I'm sorry, Dad. Guess I was talking to myself."

"Trouble?" Josh's mother asked.

Josh tried to change the subject. "What'd you decide about Kauai?"

His mother's intuition was too strong for that. She asked, "What was so important that Manuel had to see you right away?"

"I'll tell you later, okay?" Josh looked across the room at Dr. Chin. "Did you tell them to let me go back to the plane wreck?"

The pastor smiled and stood in his stocking feet. "I didn't tell them anything. I just asked questions. They made the decision."

Josh's father chuckled. "Maybe that's why Dr. Chin is considered so wise," he said. "When your mother and I answered his questions, we had our answer."

Josh felt his heart start to speed up. "Do I get to go?"

His father said, "Dr. Chin reminded me that the old Asian man we saw in the rain forest didn't bother us. In fact, when he saw us, he slipped away into that lava tube."

Mrs. Ladd mused, "I still can't understand why anyone would want to be a hermit."

Her husband told Josh, "Dr. Chin also pointed out that the man in the flight suit didn't hurt you, either, although he could have. He was right on top of us, but we didn't know it until he jumped out and ran off with your camera.

"Since we know there's no ghost, and The Phantom apparently can be explained logically, I'll rent a video camera for you. We'll go back to photograph the plane wreckage. Of course, this time we'll be prepared and not let anything happen to the camera—or us. Unfortunately, my camera isn't fixed yet or we'd take it, too."

"Wow, Dad! Thanks!" Josh started to smile, then remembered Kong's threat.

His father asked, "What's the matter, Son?"

"Uh, nothing." That wasn't true, so he instantly felt guilty for saying it. Still, he didn't want to tell his parents about Kong. Josh was aware all three adults were silently considering him. An awkward silence began to build. The pastor broke it before it became embarrassing. "I suspect your family needs some time alone. If you'll excuse me, I'll be on my way."

When Dr. Chin had gone, Mr. Ladd said firmly, "Son, your mother and I want to help you, but we can't do that unless we know what's wrong."

"It'll be okay," Josh said. "May I be excused?" He wanted to be alone in his room so he could think.

His father said softly, "No member of this family hurts alone, Son. When you've got pain, the rest of us have, too."

Josh hesitated, then spoke, hoping they'd understand. He began, "I'm in a terrible spot." Briefly, he described Manuel's message from Kong. Josh concluded, "And it's not just me, either. If I don't take Hotdog to the plane, Kong'll make life miserable for Tank and Roger, too. We'll be afraid to go to school."

Josh's father asked quietly, "Is bringing your grandmother here worth that kind of risk, Son?"

The boy hesitated, then explained. "I overheard you and Mom talking about borrowing the money to pay for Grandma's trip. But if the bank gives you the loan and you can't pay it back, you'll lose the paper."

His father's jaw muscles twitched. "That's my burden, Son, not yours."

"You said if one member of the family hurts, we all hurt. Remember?"

His father reached out and gave Josh a hug. "Nobody ever had a finer son," he said hoarsely.

Josh's mother said, "I'm still concerned about all the dangers. The jungle, two strange, old men—one who vanishes and the other who wears a World War II flying outfit and carries a sword—and now Kong's threat."

Mr. Ladd said, "Now, Mary, Kong is just trying to scare Josh."

"And doing a good job of it!" Josh thought. He could face any short-term threat, but a year of being bullied by a boy big enough to be a high school football lineman—scary!

Mrs. Ladd added, "I'm assuming the old, Oriental gentleman who disappeared into the lava tube is harmless, but we can't be sure of that. However, I'm really concerned about the one called The Phantom. I mean, he stole your camera with both of you right there!"

"But Mom, he didn't hurt us."

"I'm grateful for that, but he might not be as easy on either of you if you go back. He could be dangerous next time, especially with his sword, no matter how many of you there are."

"Mom, everything depends on getting video shots of that wreck before Hotdog does! But—are you saying I can't go?"

"I wish you would give up the idea, but I'm not changing my mind. I was just pointing out what I consider the greatest risks."

John Ladd said, "Mary, you know I wouldn't deliberately jeopardize our son's or my life. I'm sure Sam Catlett will come along, so even though Mr. Okamoto can't take time off from work right now, we have two grown men, plus Josh and probably Tank and Roger."

Josh felt his excitement rise. "We'll be safe, Mom, with so many of us. We'll go straight to the wreckage, shoot the footage, and get back quickly!"

His mother asked, "You mean, without telling Kong?"

Mr. Ladd said, "I really don't think Kong will carry out his threat."

Josh moaned inwardly, thinking differently.

John Ladd took a slow breath and concluded, "I think we've done all we can for now. Let's pray and then get to bed. We'll make the final decision in the morning."

Josh couldn't sleep. He tossed and turned until his little brother complained crossly in the darkness. Finally Josh got up and passed on bare feet down the hallway and across the living room. He unlocked the sliding door to the lanai and stepped outside in the darkness.

The warm trade winds caressed his cheeks. Moonlight bathed Diamond Head in soft light. Josh raised his eyes from the dead volcano to the stars. Everything was beautiful and peaceful, yet Josh felt the opposite inside. "What should I do?" he thought, but it was really a prayer. All his life he had been taught to rely on the Lord. "Please?" the boy whispered, looking upward. He stood there a long time, waiting for an answer. None came, so his thoughts jumped. Grandma Ladd was old and lonely. Josh missed her. They used to talk a lot when she and Grandpa visited. She sometimes offered counsel from her frayed, brown Bible or her own experience. "What would she say about Kong's threat?" Josh asked himself.

He remembered something she had said last year: "Josh, we all have fears, and sometimes they won't go away. But to do the right thing in spite of your fear shows courage and character. Remember that when you face a tough decision. And also remember all the times the Bible says, 'Fear not.' "

It sounded good at the time, but now, facing the reality of Kong's threat, Josh wasn't so sure. He thought, "I want so much to bring her over! It's not often a kid my age gets a chance to make much money, but I've got that chance if I beat Hotdog. And I should! I found the plane!"

Still, doubts flooded his mind. "What if I fail? Everything could be lost—Grandma's coming over, Dad's paper, and my health if Kong has an excuse to beat on me!"

"Fear not," the Bible said, yet Josh knew everybody was afraid sometimes. Even Jesus' disciples had run away. "Why not fear?" Josh asked himself, then remembered: "For I am with you always."

Josh went back to bed and slowly came to a decision about Kong. Yet when he awoke in the morning, the doubts seeped back like piranhas attacking his mind. "Today's my last chance!" he thought. "If I fail . . . ."

He was really fighting anxiety when finally he was aboard the short-haul jet with his father, Tank, Mr. Catlett, and Roger, who had come reluctantly. Josh knew that Roger's hesitation was because he was afraid of ghosts, yet he was facing his fear by coming along. Josh felt better knowing he wasn't alone in fighting internal conflict.

"Five to one," Josh told himself, "we'll be okay. I'll just shoot the video with Dad's rented camera and get back. Then," he tried to shake the idea, but it persisted, "I just hope Kong doesn't keep his word."

The two fathers were sitting on one side of the aisle, with Mr. Ladd at the right window. Josh, Tank, and Roger sat opposite, with Josh at the left window. He heard his father talking to his seat companion as they flew over Pearl Harbor.

"It's hard to realize that World War II began for America right down there," John Ladd said.

Tank's father replied, "I remember my dad's telling me that at the time, Japanese envoys were in Washington, D.C., still talking as if there were going to be peace."

"Meantime," Mr. Ladd said, "the Imperial Japanese Navy was steaming toward Pearl Harbor to start their sneak attack. There were three hundred fifty-four Japanese planes in these same skies on December 7, 1941.

"They struck without warning, flying in from carriers sailing about two hundred seventy miles north of here. When the attack was over a couple of hours later, the

American fleet was so badly crippled it didn't seem possible it could survive. Nearly twenty-five hundred Americans were dead and another twelve hundred wounded."

Sam Catlett asked, "How many ships and planes were lost?"

"I believe there were ninety-four warships in the harbor that morning, including eight battleships. All except the Pennsylvania were severely damaged or sunk. The Oklahoma capsized. The Arizona sank. The California and West Virginia foundered. Some destroyers and other smaller ships exploded. On land, more than one hundred American planes were also destroyed. The Japanese lost only twenty-nine aircraft."

Josh's ears perked up. "Including the one we found, huh, Dad?" he said.

His father nodded. "If three American carriers hadn't been at sea that day, along with twenty-two destroyers and cruisers, we might never have recovered from Pearl Harbor. But the American people were so outraged by the sneak attack that they rallied as one person to win the war.

"In time, those three carriers led the retaliatory strikes against Japan. Eventually, our air power and atomic bombs won, and Japan was defeated. The war was over."

Tank leaned over to Josh and whispered, "If that phantom really is an old Japanese pilot who's lived all these years by his wrecked plane, does he know the war's over?"

"I hope so!" Josh answered. "If he thinks we're the enemy. . . ." He let his sentence go unfinished.

"Don't even think that!" Tank hissed.

Roger muttered, "Better that than a ghost."

Clay Slayton, the helicopter pilot, picked up everybody at Kauai's airport and flew them toward the now-familiar blue lagoon. As the chopper cleared the last mountain and started to descend, Josh heard the pilot's surprised voice in the earphones: "Looks like your television news buddy's waiting for us."

Josh looked down and moaned, "Oh, no!"

John Ladd said, "If we land, we can't stop him from following us to the wrecked plane. Maybe we'd better turn back and try another day."

"No!" Josh spoke more sharply than he had intended. "I've got a deadline! It's got to be today or it'll be too late!"

His father protested, "But without an exclusive, Son, your video tape will be useless!"

"I've got to beat Hotdog to that footage!" Josh cried. "Otherwise, everything I want so much will be lost, and I'll have Kong on me, too!"

"But Son—"

"Please!" Josh interrupted. "Let's land! Maybe by then we can think of something."

After a moment's hesitation, the men agreed, and the

chopper started easing toward the ground. Suddenly, Josh snapped his fingers and said, "Hey! I've got it!" Quickly, he explained his plan.

When he was finished, Roger muttered, "Bruddah, you pupule!"

"It's our only chance!" Josh cried. "Please?"

His father thought a moment, then nodded. "It'll be risky, but you may be right. Let's do it!"

The three men and three boys quickly discussed what had to be done. Then the chopper's skids settled on the ground.

Josh saw Hotdog waiting. He was smiling. Josh swallowed hard, thinking, "This is my last chance! Everything depends on what happens next!"

Chapter Eleven

A STRANGE DISAPPEARANCE

The pilot stayed with the helicopter while Josh led the way toward Hotdog. Josh was followed by Roger, Tank, Mr. Ladd, and Mr. Catlett. Roger took a couple of quick steps to catch up with Josh, who was wearing a backpack and carrying a canvas shoulder bag with the rented video camera in it.

Roger lowered his voice and said, "Bruddah, I still think all you haoles pupule!"

"Maybe we are crazy," Josh said, adjusting the bag's carrying strap across his shoulders, "but you'd better hope it works. Otherwise, this is going to be the start of a whole lot of trouble!"

Josh quickened his pace and left Roger behind to approach Hotdog first. "Hi!" Josh called, trying to sound as if he had expected to find Hotdog waiting there. "You ready?"

Hotdog grinned and nodded. "Oh, I'm ready," he said, indicating a professional model, shoulder-mounted video camera. "I decided to leave the sound man and cameraman at the station. I can handle this myself." He eyed Josh's canvas bag suspiciously. "That a video camera?"

Josh patted the bag. "Rented it."

"You thought you could sneak over here and leave me out in the cold, didn't you?" the newsman said, lowering his voice. "Well, you were wrong. When you were making your plans for today, you forgot how easily sound passes through those apartments. And here I am! This is my story, understand?"

Josh said nothing.

"Frankly," Hotdog added, "I'm surprised you tried this. Kong assured me nobody'd dare go against him, including you."

Josh winced, thinking how close he had come to giving in to Kong's intimidation. If it hadn't been so important to get the video footage, he wouldn't have risked Kong's threat.

The two other boys and the two men arrived and exchanged cool greetings with Hotdog. To Josh the newsman said, "Why bring so many others along on your little adventure?"

"If we meet that man with the sword again," Josh answered, "it'll sure be good to have lots of help."

Josh's father said, "I don't appreciate your threatening my son, Mr. Grayson, and you and I are going to have a talk about that. But I realize this isn't the time or place for it. We can't keep you from coming with us, but don't think we're happy about it."

Wanting to break the tension and get on with the search, Josh said to Hotdog, "I'm surprised Kong's not with you."

"That local is scared of ghosts," Hotdog said, looking relieved at the change of subject. "He wouldn't come. Well, let's get moving. Which way, Kid?"

Josh hated being called "kid." He said quietly, "Call me Josh."

"Kid, Josh, whatever," Hotdog said with a wave of his free hand. "Take me to that wreck! And if that old geezer with the sword jumps us, all of you keep him busy so I can get some action shots."

Josh expected to see Hotdog grin to show he was joking. He wasn't even smiling. Josh felt angry words boil up inside, but he stopped himself from saying anything when he saw his father's jaw muscles twitch. Josh knew that meant his dad was struggling to avoid saying something he might regret.

Aloud, Mr. Ladd said, "Son, since you've been here twice before, how about leading the way?"

Josh nodded and hurried past the volcanic shaft shaped like a giant spear point. As the group entered the jungle, the humidity settled over them like a hot blanket. Almost at once, Josh felt beads of moisture form under his armpits. His shirt would soon be soaked, especially where the backpack with the flashlight pressed against him.

His nose wrinkled at the smell of rotting guavas on the ground. Swarms of gnats and mosquitos buzzed annoyingly around his ears. He brushed them away and glanced up. The overhead canopy of trees made deep shadows from which unseen birds called alarm warnings.

Hotdog grumbled, "Well, with all those birds screeching loud enough to wake the dead, The Phantom will know we're coming. What great footage I'll get if he charges us with that sword!"

Josh glanced at the others. He could see each was annoyed by the arrogant reporter's attitude. Hotdog added, "Of course, nobody should get hurt."

Josh said, "All of you had better wait here a minute while I scout ahead and get my bearings."

Hotdog called, "Don't slip off and leave us behind, Josh. We wouldn't want anything to happen to you!" He made his comment sound light-hearted, but it held a veiled warning.

"I'll stay in sight," Josh assured him. "I don't want to be alone if that phantom or whoever is waiting for us."

Josh smiled to himself and began looking for the monofilament fish line his father had played out on their last trip into the jungle. It was almost invisible, but finally Josh's sharp eyes saw it.

He sighed gently, thinking, "I'm glad that old Oriental man didn't take it. Now I'll run out a second line so Hotdog can find his way back when I manage to slip off to the wreck."

The boy turned and walked back to the others. The big problem would be carrying out the hurried plan made as the helicopter was landing. Josh, his father, and Roger had to somehow slip away from Hotdog. Then they would hurry to the wrecked plane, where Josh would shoot new footage before they all rushed back to the helicopter and on to Honolulu.

Mr. Catlett had agreed to stay with Hotdog so he'd be safe in case the swordsman appeared. And Mr. Catlett had wanted Tank to stay with him. Tank hadn't liked the idea of having to stay behind, but Roger was the opposite. "I don't mind staying," he had said, glancing anxiously around.

Josh suspected Roger was privately afraid there might really be a ghost in the jungle, but he didn't want to admit he was scared. So he had agreed to go along with the plan.

"Now," Josh told himself, "the next step is to give Hotdog the slip. But how?" There hadn't been time on the chopper to figure that out.

Josh turned and walked back to his father. "Dad, you got that line?"

"Right here." Mr. Ladd handed over a large spool of fish line.

"Thanks." Josh took the spool and tied the line's end to a vine hanging chin high.

Hotdog exclaimed, "So that's how you got in and out of here the other day!"

Josh smiled. "It was my father's idea. This'll make sure we all get back safely—I mean, in case we get separated or anything."

He turned and pushed into the jungle, letting the nearly invisible line flow off the spool. He deliberately stayed a few feet away from the first line, but close enough to see it from time to time. Josh told himself, "I just hope Hotdog doesn't see the old line. He might wonder why I'm laying this new one instead of following the original."

When Josh got close to the wreck, he planned to hand the new spool to Tank, who would lead Hotdog away from the wreck after Josh disappeared. Josh would go to the plane, get his footage, then follow the first line back to safety. "But I've got to get away fast!" Josh concluded to himself.

He stopped and looked back. Everyone was spread out in single file. Hotdog was closest to Josh, followed by the two fathers. Tank was next-to-last, and Roger brought up the rear.

Satisfied, Josh returned to breaking trail and playing out the line. He stopped occasionally to make sure he was running parallel to the first line. Then he pushed on, his heart speeding up.

"Soon we'll be coming up to where we saw the old man disappear into the lava tube," Josh told himself. "I wonder what we'll see when we shine a flashlight into it?"

As they pushed deeper into the rain forest, Josh was surprised to see how many lava tubes he'd overlooked before. They were scattered about, totally covered with jungle growth. Only by looking carefully could he recognize the tube openings. Most were much smaller than the one where the old Oriental had vanished.

Josh glanced anxiously ahead and thought, "There's that tree with the top out, so we're getting close to the wreck. I've got to slip away from Hotdog. But how?"

He suspected his father was thinking the same thing, as were Tank, Roger, and Mr. Catlett. Since none had said or done anything, however, they must not have been able to come up with an idea, either.

"Think!" Josh told himself. "Think fast!" Everything depended on being separated from Hotdog, and soon. Once Josh had his new shots and he was back at the helicopter with his dad and Roger, the pilot would fly them directly to the Lihue airport.

"We've got our return tickets to Honolulu," Josh reminded himself. "When we get there, Dad'll call the news director at the television station and tell him about the video tape. Dad thinks the station will jump at our offer. They can air the tape free locally if they'll arrange the sale to the network and cable news."

Hotdog called, "How much farther?"

"Not much." Josh glanced ahead and realized time was running out. The trail was coming up fast. Once on it, Hotdog might see the plane. If that happened, everything Josh wanted would be lost.

Hotdog shifted the heavy video camera balanced on his shoulder. "I hope you're right," he said, "because carrying this through the jungle is mighty hard work."

"I'll carry your camera a while, Grayson," Sam Catlett said.

"No, thanks! I've got to be ready to start shooting fast! Remember, if that guy in the yellow boots shows up with his sword—"

"We know!" Mr. Ladd interrupted.

Josh decided to stall for time while trying to think of a way to slip away from Hotdog. Turning around, breathing hard from pushing his way through undergrowth and vines and stepping over logs and exposed roots, he said, "This camera's heavy, too. Let's take a break."

The others willingly accepted the suggestion. They quickly sat on stumps, logs, or the jungle floor. Josh's father didn't rest, however, but passed the others to approach his son. Keeping his back turned and lowering his voice, he said, "I think I recognize some landmarks. Are we getting close?"

Josh nodded and turned so the others couldn't see his lips. He whispered, "We're almost there! But how're we going to get away from Hotdog?"

"I've worked that out."

"You have?"

"Yes, but I've been thinking. Watch out for whoever snatched your camera the other day. I don't think he'll do anything with all of us here, but we can't be sure."

"Especially if he brings his sword," Josh said, glancing anxiously around.

"And keep an eye open for the old Oriental, Son. I think it was right up ahead that he vanished into that lava tube."

Josh nodded. "It's close, all right. Are we going to take a flashlight and look into the tube?"

"Yes, but only after we get your taping done. I'm eager to see how the old man disappeared so easily."

"Nothing matters if I can't get away from Hotdog soon!"

Mr. Ladd leaned close and smiled. He started to whisper something just as Josh looked back along the single file of men and boys. His father turned to look the same way. "What's the matter, Son?"

Josh raised his voice in alarm. "Where's Roger?"

Everyone turned to look back where Roger had been the last in line. He wasn't there.

"Roger?" Josh called. "Where are you?"

There was no answer. He had vanished without a sound!

Chapter Twelve

HOSTAGES!

Everyone looked around and called his name, but Roger didn't answer. Josh pushed past the others to Roger's spot at the end of the single file. Desperately, Josh glanced at the ground and then around the jungle. "Nothing!" he exclaimed. "Not a sign of him!"

Tank cried, "He couldn't just disappear!"

Josh said, "He was right behind you! Didn't you hear him?"

"No."

"Didn't you hear anything, Tank?"

"I'm sorry—nothing. Not a sound!"

Tank's father ran up and joined the boys in looking around for some clue to Roger's disappearance. Josh's father did not join in.

"No sign of a struggle," Mr. Catlett said. "No piece of clothing. Nothing!"

Josh urged, "Keep looking!" He lifted his eyes from the jungle floor to the surrounding rain forest, shaking his head. "I don't believe this is happening!"

He turned toward Hotdog and stopped in surprise. "What're you doing?" he demanded sharply.

"Shooting the scene," Hotdog said, his right eye against the rubber viewfinder. The big camera was balanced on his right shoulder, while his right hand supported the front portion.

Tank's father exploded, "Cut that out and come help us!" He had said very little on the trip, but now Josh understood how he could manage a department store. There was authority in his voice.

"Sure," Hotdog replied, removing his cheek from against the camera. "I've shot enough anyway."

Josh's father said evenly, "Let's spread out and look for Roger, but stay within sight or sound of each other. Here, Sam, you take this." Mr. Ladd took the spool of monofilament line from Josh and handed it to Tank's father.

Josh turned to look into the dense undergrowth to his right. He was aware that his heart was beating rapidly, and his mouth was suddenly dry.

His father took a few quick steps and called, "Wait up, Son!" The boy stopped as his father ran up to him. Mr. Ladd whispered, "Josh, you slip into the jungle and get to the plane! In a minute I'll also slip away, cross to the other line, and meet you there!"

"But Roger—"

"Shh! He's giving us our chance to beat Grayson!"

Josh blinked in surprise. "You mean Roger

deliberately—"

His father nodded emphatically. "He and I worked it out a while ago. We didn't have a chance to tell the others, because Grayson might have gotten suspicious. Now move! But be careful!"

Josh heaved a big sigh of relief.

"Hurry, Son!"

Josh nodded and shifted the canvas carrying bag to where he could grip it with both hands. He pushed through the head-high jungle growth. In seconds, he was out of sight of all the others and heading straight for the place he had last seen their original fishing line. A moment later, heart thumping with excitement, he found it. "Now!" he told himself, turning to follow the line. "A few more steps to the trail, and then the plane!"

Soon he was at the crash site. He reached down and unzipped the canvas bag to remove the video camera. Dropping the bag beside the trail, he hoisted the camera to his shoulder.

"Start with a wide angle shot," he reminded himself. "Get the whole scene, then zoom in on the fuselage." He closed his left eye and placed the right against the black rubber viewfinder. He was breathing so hard and his heart was thumping so loudly that he felt the camera moving slightly. "Hold your breath!" he told himself.

He pressed the red "on" button with his right thumb and then released it. The tape would continue to run until he pressed the red button again. The unit automatically set the aperture to permit the right amount of light to reach the tape.

Even though his right ear was against the camera housing, the operation was so silent that Josh barely heard a slight hum. That meant the tape was turning, moving from one spoollike part of the cassette to the other.

"Good! Good!" Josh whispered to himself. "Everything's nice and clear. Now zoom in." His right forefinger pressed the zoom control. The viewfinder picture began to slide silently forward.

He heard a sound behind him. "Looks great, Dad!" he whispered without looking up. When the zoom-in shot went out of focus on the faded rising sun insignia, Josh reversed the process. The zoom withdrew, giving Josh a wide-angle shot. He started to press the "off" button, then changed his mind, keeping his right eye pressed against the viewfinder.

"Just a minute, Dad," he said in a hoarse stage whisper, even though he felt Hotdog was too far away to hear. "I'm going to pan around the jungle to get the location on tape. When I come around to you, how about walking past me and up to the plane? That'll give me some good action."

Panning slowly, as he had been taught, Josh held the camera steady and carefully moved it in a wide circle. Through the viewfinder he saw the tree canopy overhead, the trailing vines, the dense, green underbrush, and the twisted, exposed roots of trees.

"Now, Dad," he whispered, "I'm coming around to

you. Don't look right at the camera. Look beyond me at the wreck, then start walking—" Josh stopped so suddenly he jerked the camera. He opened his left eye and removed the other from the viewfinder.

His father wasn't there.

Instead, an old, Oriental man stood silently before him in yellow boots and ancient flying clothes. He held a sword, with the point aimed at Josh.

Josh opened his mouth to yell, but the long blade moved slightly. He closed his mouth so suddenly that his teeth clicked together. The sword point moved sharply to the left—once, twice. The man's helmeted head snapped emphatically in the same direction.

Speaking from a suddenly dry mouth that seemed to have a piece of wood for a tongue, Josh said, "You want me to go that way?"

The sword point moved again, more emphatically.

"I can't!" Josh protested, even though he realized the old man couldn't understand him. "You see, my father'll be here in a minute, and he—"

He was interrupted by a warning exclamation in Japanese. At the same instant, the sword slashed upward.

"Okay! Okay! I'm going!" Josh started to turn in the indicated direction, but he stole a quick glance the way he'd come. He moaned inwardly, "Dad! Where are you?"

He felt the camera jerked from his shoulder and automatically protested, "Hey! That's rented!"

His captor examined the camera. Josh suddenly

realized he hadn't pushed the "off" button. The camera was still running, which meant the black microphone mounted above the lens was still recording, too.

The realization of what was being recorded struck Josh with a sharp jolt. He twisted slightly to see how the old man was carrying the camera but stopped at a warning grunt. A minute or so later, Josh walked behind a six-foot-tall ti plant that hid the entrance to a four-foot-high lava tube.

The boy turned uncertainly, but the sword point lightly tapped the tube's entrance. Josh protested, "You want me to—" He didn't finish the sentence, because a glance at his captor confirmed it was exactly what he wanted.

Josh said, "Wait! I've got a flashlight in my pack!" The sword was raised in silent warning. Holding up both hands, palms outward, Josh said, "Okay! Okay! It was just a suggestion."

Reluctantly, Josh bent and entered the dark tube. He placed his hands against the rough interior walls and felt his way along. His feet touched something, and he almost fell. Heart beating wildly, Josh dropped to his knees and touched whatever had almost tripped him.

"Roger!" he exclaimed.

"Umm!" The answering noise instantly confirmed Josh's guess. But the muffled tone meant Roger was gagged.

Josh's eyes slowly adjusted to the gloomy interior of the tube. He heard their captor say something sharply to

Roger in Japanese. Roger's head moved in a slight nod. The old man reached down and removed Roger's gag. Then he turned and hurried back to the tube's entrance. He stood there in silhouette, apparently listening for anybody who might be following.

Josh whispered to Roger, "What happened? Weren't you supposed to just pretend to disappear so we could get away from Hotdog?"

"I was, but I hadn't gone twenty feet before this guy grabbed me from behind. He clamped one hand over my mouth so I couldn't yell. And he's surprisingly strong for such an old guy! I started to struggle anyway, and he showed me the sword. So I decided not to yell and to go the way he pointed."

"Did he say anything?"

"Yeah! He seems to think I speak Japanese, so he babbled something about—"

"But you do speak Japanese!" Josh interrupted.

"Only a little! I understand it pretty well because my Grandmother Yamaguchi talks it so much, but—"

"What'd he say?" Josh broke in again, watching the shadowy figure at the tube's entrance.

"A lot of things. He thought I might be a prisoner of war, so he wanted to rescue me. But he wasn't sure. That's why he grabbed me. He also claims he's the pilot of the wrecked plane! That'd mean he's been living here all alone for about fifty years. Frankly, I don't think he's got all his marbles, Josh! I mean, wearing that hot suit in all this heat and humidity!"

Josh nodded, thinking his father would have said, "He's mentally disturbed." Aloud, Josh said, "Maybe he wears it as his uniform in dealing with what he figures is the enemy. Did he say what he's going to do with us?"

"No, he just—here he comes again!"

The pilot gently laid the sword down and bent over Roger. *"Anata no onamae wa?"*

Josh was startled to realize he understood the Japanese question: "What is your honorable name?" It was something Roger's mother had taught him.

Roger answered the old man, "Roger Okamoto desu." Roger moved his head toward Josh. "Josh Ladd desu."

The old man nodded with satisfaction. "Honda desu, pairotto."

Josh blinked and whispered, "Did he say his name is Honda?"

"Yes. It's a very old Japanese name that means 'main rice paddy.' 'Pairotto' is 'pilot.' "

"What's he want with us?" Josh managed to ask, glancing at the sword resting beside Mr. Honda.

"I can't think how to say that in Japanese!"

"Well, try," Josh whispered, "while I see if I can think of a way to get us out of this mess!"

Roger hesitantly began speaking in Japanese, periodically mixing in English where he couldn't remember the other language.

Josh started thinking, "Dad'll be at the plane wreck by

now, but he's got no way of knowing where I am. Even if he walked right by here, he'd never see this lava tube with that big ti plant hiding the entrance. I'll bet he's about frantic by now!"

But Josh couldn't think what to do before Roger spoke again in English. "He's got a wild story, Josh!"

"How so?"

"As near as I can make it out, he claims he didn't believe in the war. He'd been to America and studied a while at UCLA, about 1937, but he's forgotten most of his English and he's even rusty in Japanese. He's had nobody to talk to all these years."

"What about us?"

"I'm coming to that. When he flew in to attack Pearl Harbor in 1941, he pretended he had engine trouble and tried to turn back to the carrier. But he flew into the clouds on this mountain and crashed."

"You're kidding!"

"That's what I understood him to say."

"How'd he survive the crash?"

"Parachuted at the last second. He decided to live here because he'd disgrace his family if they knew he had failed in his duty to attack the enemy. He's been here ever since."

"Do you believe him?"

"I don't know, Josh. Oh, he also says you and your father caught him by surprise the other day. So he slipped into the lava tube, put on his old flying clothes, and came back to grab your camera. He's kept the flying outfit, saying he wants to die in it."

Josh nodded. His great grandfather had kept his doughboy uniform from World War I so he could be buried in it. Aloud, Josh mused, "So there's only one person, not two. And Mr. Honda must be The Phantom."

Roger sighed and said, "I'm glad there's no ghost."

Josh repeated his original question. "What's he going to do with us?"

"He said he doesn't know. If the war's been over for years, as I told him, we're not the enemy. But he can't let us go because we'll bring more people, and he wants to die out here the way he lived: alone."

"I can't believe that!"

"I'm just telling you what he said. He'd disgrace his family in Japan after what he did at Pearl Harbor. Oh, he also figured out how your camera works."

"The one he grabbed from me?"

"Yes. He said he was always good at such things. So he fooled with the camera until he found out how to see the cassette played back in the viewfinder."

"Then he knows what I've got on the tape?" Josh started to add, "Wait'll he sees what I've got on the one he just took from me!" Before Josh could speak, however, Roger spoke again.

"He wanted to know what you were going to do with it, so I told him, but he doesn't understand what television means. He only knows radio. He also claims he's got a bad heart and expects to die soon. After that, he doesn't care about the tapes."

Josh's alarm grew rapidly. "Does that mean he's not going to let us go as long as he lives?"

"Sounded that way to me! Our fathers will see that a search is made for us, but they'd never find us in these lava tubes. Mr. Honda says they even carry off smoke from his campfires, so nobody's ever seen any sign of him. Well, except a few times when he was raiding the 'enemy,' as he called them, down near the villages."

Panic started to seize Josh, but then an idea formed in his mind. "Ask him if he would go back to Japan if he could go as a hero instead of in disgrace," Josh said. "Ask him if he'd like to bring honor to his family."

Roger shrugged, obviously not understanding what Josh had in mind, but he spoke to the pilot in Japanese.

Their captor bowed smartly, exclaimed, "Hai!" and then rattled off something else.

Roger translated. "He says yes, but that it's not possible."

"Maybe it is. Tell him we can help him clear his name and bring honor to his family if he'll let us go now."

Roger tried, then translated the old man's response. "He says, 'How can two boys do such a thing?'"

"Tell him that when his story is told on worldwide television, he won't be in disgrace, because Japan and America are friends, and most Japanese now believe their country should never have attacked Pearl Harbor. People in both countries will also respect him for doing what he thought was right.

"I think, too, that the Japanese will respect the sacrifice he's made these last forty-some years for the sake of honor and will feel he's redeemed himself anyway. It's time for him to go home, and I'm sure he'll be treated like a hero."

"But Josh, he doesn't understand TV!"

"Tell him anyway!"

Roger did, then said, "He seems doubtful and a little confused, especially since he's just been told the war is over. But he's willing to take a chance. He said one of us can go now if we first make sure that anyone with a camera—especially the man who came with us—doesn't come near here again."

"He's got to let us both go, Roger!"

"He won't go along with that!"

Josh frowned, then snapped his fingers. "I know! Ask him if we can get everyone who came with us today to leave immediately, will he let us go?"

"Hotdog won't leave! When we tell him about Mr. Honda here, he'll be wild to get the story on tape."

"Not if my idea works! Ask Mr. Honda fast, please!"

Roger translated and then turned back to Josh. "He says yes, but on two conditions. Only one of us can go to convince the others to leave. The other stays as a hostage to make sure the first boy doesn't play any tricks on him. And he's got to see that Hotdog is really gone."

"Tell him he can go along and watch. Oh, yes, one thing more. Tell him we'll need both the cameras to clear his name. But we promise we won't tell anyone where he is unless he changes his mind about staying a hermit."

Roger obeyed, then gave Josh the pilot's answer. "He doesn't understand how you can make everyone leave, but he says if you'll get rid of Hotdog, his camera, and the others, he'll give back your cameras and let us both go. That's providing we give our honorable word that he won't disgrace his family."

Josh was a little surprised Honda was being so agreeable. Was it a trick? He asked Roger, "Do you think we can trust him? Why is he so quick to go along with my plan, anyway?"

Roger shrugged and said, "Maybe it's because he's old and thinks he's going to die. Maybe he's lonely after all these years by himself and wants to be friendly. Maybe he's desperate for a way to return to Japan with honor. Or maybe he's just more trusting of us because we're boys instead of grown men."

"Any of those make sense, I guess. Okay. I'll tell you my plan, Roger, and then you go."

When Josh had briefly explained, Roger exclaimed, "You planty pupule, Bruddah!"

"We don't have a choice unless you've got a better idea."

Roger sighed. "Okay, but you'd better go instead of me. I sure hope your idea works!"

Josh nodded and said, "Okay, now tell him I need to borrow his yellow boots and flying clothes."

Chapter Thirteen

A DESPERATE CHARGE

Josh felt awkward in Mr. Honda's heavy flying suit, helmet, and bright yellow boots. When he took his first step, he almost fell. He told Roger, "I feel like the boy David trying to wear King Saul's armor to fight Goliath. But my plan won't work unless I have this outfit on."

Josh stumbled as he followed his captor through a series of unlit lava tubes. He wished he had suggested using his flashlight, but the old man moved effortlessly through the darkened interiors until they emerged in the rain forest. There he stopped, cocked his head to listen, and stood still as a stump.

Josh did likewise, hoping to catch some sign of his father or the others. He didn't see or hear anything.

For the first time, Josh got a good look at his captor in full daylight. He looked like any of the old, Oriental men Josh had seen throughout the islands, except for the thin, scraggly beard. There was nothing about him to suggest he was a Japanese warrior who hadn't known World

War II was over until an hour or so before.

He now wore faded khaki pants, a tattered, blue-and-white aloha shirt, and sandals made from an old tire. He carried a sword about three feet long. Mr. Honda had explained to Roger that except for the sword, these items had been "liberated" from a supposed-enemy farmhouse down in a valley.

Josh guessed what Mr. Honda meant was that he'd stolen the stuff. He'd admitted to Roger that he'd taken many things he'd needed over the years. However, since Mr. Honda thought he was taking from his enemies, he didn't consider it stealing at all. He was freeing the things he needed from the enemy, he had said with a smile. The sword he had made by hand.

As Josh stood there, eyes and ears strained to their utmost, the jungle humidity struck him. He began to perspire under all the heavy clothing. "I've got to do this fast or I'll smother in this outfit!" he told himself.

Off to their right, a bird's alarm call caused the old Japanese to swivel his head and stare. He began to move as silently as a shadow toward the bird. Josh followed, but the yellow boots made him sound like a giant clumping through the jungle.

His captor turned, gave the boy an annoyed frown, and waved the sword point at the boots. Josh shrugged, indicating he couldn't be any quieter. Mr. Honda grunted disapprovingly and continued through the dense underbrush. Josh followed, lifting the clumsy boots and setting them down as gently as possible.

As his eyes roamed the area in search of his father, Josh caught sight of something vaguely familiar. "Hey!" he thought. "We're going toward the edge of the jungle! Yeah! I can see the top of that lone banyan where Tank, Roger, and I swung over the ravine!"

Mr. Honda stopped suddenly and pointed. Josh looked carefully in the same direction but saw nothing. As he was trying to figure out how to make his captor understand that, a familiar voice called out from the jungle's depths. "Hey, Catlett! Where're you and your kid?"

"Hotdog!" Josh thought. "If he'll just keep talking...."

The Japanese pilot wordlessly handed Josh the sword. Josh almost dropped it in surprise. He felt the weight of the glistening, steel blade and realized he suddenly had a weapon. Glancing at Mr. Honda's eyes, he saw the old warrior was trusting him. He looked back at the sword and knew he could not betray that trust.

When Josh raised his eyes again, Mr. Honda was gone. He had disappeared like a puff of smoke.

Josh knew their captor was watching him, but he thought of Roger, waiting back in the darkness of the lava tube. He held the sword high and pushed through the jungle toward Hotdog. He was committed to his plan for freeing Roger and himself.

"Wonder where Dad is?" Josh mused. His father was supposed to have made his way to the wreck. If he had, what had he done when he realized Josh wasn't there? Would he have dared search alone and risk getting lost? Or would he have returned to the others?

"The main thing," Josh told himself, "is that Hotdog doesn't know anything about Roger's original plan to 'get lost.' "

The boy's mind jumped. "I hope this works," Josh thought as he plodded along. "When everybody sees me in this outfit, I wish there was some way I could let them know it's me—except Hotdog. But there's no way I can do that, so I've got to take a chance my friends won't clobber me, thinking they've got The Phantom. I probably couldn't outrun them."

Josh's doubts began to nibble at his mind again, causing a scary feeling inside. "If I get caught or don't get rid of Hotdog, Mr. Honda'll take Roger and disappear even deeper into the rain forest! I'll never get my cameras back, either! That'd be the end of everything!"

Josh slowed as he neared the last sheltering line of undergrowth. He eased through until there were only two chin-high ti plants between him and the clearing with the banyan tree and the deep gorge.

Hotdog's voice called out, "That dumb Roger, getting lost like that! Now Josh's lost, too! This is spoiling everything for me!"

Mr. Catlett snapped, "Oh, stop complaining!"

Josh wanted to cheer Tank's dad, but he was more interested in seeing where everyone was, especially his own father.

Josh eased closer, trying to see without being seen. He spied Hotdog first. Grayson was sitting on the ground about twenty feet from the banyan tree's main trunk, his knees drawn up under his chin. His face showed weariness and frustration. But he was still the newsman, for the heavy video camera rested beside him, cradled between his right arm and his side.

Continuing to look for Tank and Mr. Catlett, Josh located them at the edge of the rain forest, moving through chest-high brush about a dozen feet apart.

"They're still searching for Roger and me!" Josh told himself. "Wonder where Dad—there! He must not have been able to sneak away." At the sight of his father, moving through the jungle a little farther in, the boy wanted to call out. But he didn't dare.

Josh took a deep breath and swallowed hard, preparing himself for what had to be done. But before he could move, he heard his father's voice. "This is the last spool of fishing line," he said. "We've got to turn around or we'll never find our way back."

Just then Josh heard a startled exclamation from Hotdog. The boy snapped his gaze back to the newsman. He was scrambling to his feet, looking straight at Josh. Hotdog cried in a hoarse stage whisper, "Look! Look, everybody! It's the phantom pilot!"

Josh's mouth suddenly went dry. He started to draw back to the safety of the rain forest. Then he stopped, remembering what he had to do. "Now!" Josh thought. "Lord, give me courage, please!"

The boy took a deep breath and burst from between the sheltering ti plants into the open. "Banzai!" he yelled, raising the sword high above his head and charging straight toward Hotdog.

The clumsy boots almost made Josh fall on his first step, but he regained his balance and kept running. "Banzai!" Josh shrieked again, swinging the sword. "Banzai!"

He had expected Hotdog to jump and run in panic. He didn't. Regardless of Josh's low opinion of the man, Hotdog was a newsman. He hoisted the heavy video camera to his shoulder. "Stop him, you guys!" Hotdog yelled, dropping his head so his right eye was on the viewfinder. "Hurry! I've got to get these shots!"

Josh heard crashing sounds off to the side as his father, Tank, and Mr. Catlett rushed out of the jungle.

"Oh, Lord, please!" Josh muttered, running toward Hotdog as fast as he could without falling on his face. Aloud, Josh shrieked again, "Banzai!"

What Hotdog saw in the viewfinder must have quickly become too much for his nerves. He suddenly lowered the camera and looked around desperately for a way to escape.

Josh heard Tank yell, "The vine! Hotdog, grab a vine and swing across the canyon like we told you we did!"

Hotdog took one fast look over his shoulder at the

nearing figure, then whirled and gripped the camera with his left hand. He looked up, grabbed a dangling vine with his free hand, and began to sprint straight toward the ravine.

"Two hands!" Tank yelled. "You'll never make it jumping with just one!"

Hotdog didn't seem to hear. He reached the end of the vine and leaped. His momentum carried him up in an arc above the ravine.

Josh slowed his charge without thinking. He remembered how far down it was to the bottom of that gorge. Lowering his sword unconsciously, he wanted to yell, "Two hands!"

It was too late. Hotdog screamed, "I'm slipping!"

"Let go of the camera!" Josh's father yelled. "Grab the vine with both—"

Josh thought, "Oh, no! Hotdog's going to fall, and it's my fault!"

The heavy camera fell straight down and out of sight. Hotdog's suddenly free left hand grabbed for the vine over his head. Then he was over the gorge. He landed in a rolling fall on the far side of the ravine.

Josh wanted to let out a happy yell, but he checked himself. He glanced back and to his left. His father, Tank, and Mr. Catlett were running toward him. He whirled away and plunged into the jungle, knowing his plan wasn't yet complete.

Josh heard his father yell, "Hey! Wait! We want to talk

to you! We won't hurt you!"

Mr. Catlett shouted, "The war's over! We're friends!"

Josh wanted to shout, "It's me! Josh!" But Roger was still a hostage, so Josh plowed ahead. Then without warning, he tripped and fell hard, dropping the sword. Instantly, hearing the pursuit behind him, Josh scrambled to his feet. "Lord," he prayed, "help me and Roger!"

Josh scooped up the sword and clumped noisily through the underbrush. His breath started coming in ragged gasps. He glanced around desperately, thinking, "I'm going to get lost! Where is Mr. Honda?"

The boy stumbled and started to fall again, but strong hands grabbed him by the upper right arm and broke his fall. Josh recovered his balance and turned, breathing hard, to see the old pilot beside him. Mr. Honda smiled, bowed formally, and said softly, *"Domo arigato gozaimasu."*

"You're welcome," Josh said without realizing he remembered this was the polite term for "Thank you very much."

Josh handed over the sword. He guessed the old pilot was pleased. Josh whispered, "Roger Okamoto!"

"Hai!" Mr. Honda replied. He turned swiftly and led the way through the jungle.

Josh breathed a sigh of gratitude. "Thanks, Lord!" he whispered.

Half an hour later, the old warrior had led Josh and Roger to the plane. Both video cameras were handed to

Josh. He looked at Roger and said, "Tell him we won't show the tapes until our fathers and friends have started helping clear his name. Then he can go home to Japan without disgrace."

Roger translated quickly.

The old pilot bowed to both boys, then smiled and said softly, "Sayonara."

Josh knew the word meant "Good-bye." He smiled at Mr. Honda and said, "Sayonara." Then he handed a camera to Roger as they started back toward the helicopter.

Hardly a month had passed before the Ladd family drove to the Honolulu airport and bought four flower leis at the stands by the parking lot. Chattering with excitement, they hurried through the terminal and out onto one of the long, open-air, concrete concourses.

Tiffany cried, "I can hardly wait!"

"Me, too," her father said.

Josh's mother, dressed in a fitted, blue-and-white-printed holokuu,* added, "Should be any minute now."

Josh didn't say anything. He felt the small droplets of moisture from the fragrant plumeria lei gently swinging from his extended right forearm. He was too excited to talk. So many things had happened!

Kong believed it was his threat that had forced Josh to lead Hotdog toward the crashed plane. It wasn't Josh's fault, Kong figured, that "dah ghost" had caused Hotdog to drop the camera without getting the video footage he wanted.

Hotdog stoutly claimed he was attacked by The Phantom. The television station management took a different view, especially about the ruined camera. Hotdog angrily returned to the Mainland.

Josh's father hadn't needed to borrow from the bank. The video tapes had earned far more money from broadcast and cable networks than Josh had dreamed possible. The cassettes were sensational news, especially since Josh had left the borrowed camera running. The old Japanese warrior's words had been recorded, including his explanation of what had happened to him since Pearl Harbor.

Mr. Honda returned to Japan as an honored hero who had returned from the dead. His family, especially the grandson he had never known about, was proud of him.

John Ladd did have a talk with Josh, however, about their use of deception to keep Hotdog from getting footage of the plane and Mr. Honda. "My plan for Roger to pretend to disappear wasn't the most honest way to deal with the situation, was it?" Mr. Ladd said.

"No," Josh answered, "and neither was my pretending to be Mr. Honda and scaring Hotdog. But we were under pressure and didn't know what else to do. In my case, Roger's and my freedom seemed to be in danger, so I did the first thing I thought of."

"I understand that, Son, but deception of any kind is not a good policy. Let's talk to Dr. Chin about how we might have responded differently in that situation, okay?"

Josh nodded. "Yes, Dad."

Now Josh felt good. Everything had turned out well, and Grandma Ladd had been right about fear. It helped to remember why the Bible said so often, "Fear not." When the Lord was with you, you could do things you hadn't thought possible.

"Here it comes!" Nathan shouted, pointing skyward. "Out to sea, just passing Diamond Head!"

Josh and the rest of his family shaded their eyes with their hands. The jumbo jet looked like a silver-sided shark moving effortlessly through an inverted, blue sea.

"It'll be great having Grandma here!" Nathan added. "Really great, huh, Josh?"

Josh nodded. "Really great!" he said, dropping a hand on his little brother's shoulder.

As the jet touched down and rolled to a stop, Josh wondered if Grandma Ladd would like to go on an adventure with them. Knowing her spirit, he guessed she would.

The Ladd family, with leis draped over their forearms, began moving down the concourse toward the gate. Josh could hardly wait to present Grandma with a lei and tell her all the exciting things they could do together. He was sure she would love that.

"Who knows?" Josh thought. "Our most exciting adventure might be yet to come!"

GLOSSARY

Chapter One

Banyan tree: *(ban-yun* tree*)* A tree of the mulberry family that extends shoots from its branches that drop to the ground and root, forming secondary trunks. A single banyan tree may cover several acres of ground.

Banzai: *(bahn-zi)* The battle cry used by World War II Japanese military men when they charged the enemy.

Bruddah: *(brud-duh)* Pidgin English for "brother."

Da kine: *(dah-kine)* Pidgin English for "the kind." This is more of an expression and is therefore not usually translated literally.

Fluke: *(flook)* A parasitic flatworm that can carry many diseases.

Guava: *(gwav-ah)* A sweet yellow fruit grown in tropical areas.

Kauai: *(ka-why)* A Hawaiian island northwest of Oahu (where Honolulu is located). Kauai is thought by many to be the most photogenic of the islands.

Koolau Range: *(koh-oh-low* range*)* The volcanic mountains that rise directly behind Honolulu.

Menehune: *(meh-nah-hoo-nay)* A race of tiny people in Hawaiian legends who are credited with building many temples, fishponds, and roads. They worked only at night, and if their work was not completed in one night, it remained unfinished.

Mount Waialeale: *(*mount *why-ahl-ee-ahl-ee)* The 5,148-foot-high mountain and extinct volcano that created the island of Kauai. It is the world's wettest spot, receiving between 500 and 600 inches of rain annually.

Pidgin English: *(pidj-uhn* english*)* A simplified version of English. It was originally used in the Orient for communication between people who spoke different languages.

Pupule: *(poo-poo-lay)* Hawaiian for "crazy."

Ti: *(tee)* A plant with long, slender, green leaves that are used to make skirts for the hula dancers who entertain visitors to Hawaii. Although many Mainlanders and songs refer to the dancers' wearing "grass skirts," the skirts are usually made from ti leaves.

Wikiwiki: *(wee-kee-wee-kee)* Hawaiian for "hurry."

Chapter Two

Anaconda: *(an-uh-kon-duh)* A large, semiaquatic

snake of the boa family that crushes its prey in its coils.

Kokua: *(ko-koo-ah)* Hawaiian for "help."

Malihini: *(mah-lee-hee-nee)* Hawaiian for "newcomer."

Planty: *(plant-ee)* Pidgin English for "plenty."

Chapter Three

Be-still tree: A short tree with dense green foliage and bright yellow flowers that fold up at night.

Haole: *(how-lee)* A Hawaiian word originally meaning "stranger" but now used to mean Caucasians, or white people.

Kamuela: *(kah-mah-way-lah)* Hawaiian for "Samuel."

Pele: *(pay-lay)* A Hawaiian goddess of fire who supposedly caused volcanoes to erupt when she was angry.

Stills: Nonmoving pictures, such as snapshots.

Chapter Four

Akamai: *(ah-kah-my)* Hawaiian for "smart, intelligent."

Board and batten house: A house with a particular style of siding. Wide boards or sheets of lumber are set vertically, and the joints are covered by small strips of wood (battens).

Huhu: *(hoo-hoo)* Hawaiian for "angry."

Malasada: *(mahl-ah-sahd-a)* A Portuguese pastry like a doughnut without a hole and covered with sugar. Malasadas are best eaten hot.

Oleanders: *(oh-lee-an-derz)* Poisonous evergreen shrubs with fragrant flowers in white, pink, or red.

Pilikia: *(pee-lee-kee-ah)* Hawaiian for "trouble."

Plumeria: *(ploo-mar-ee-ah)* A shrub or small tree that produces large, fragrant blossoms often used to make leis (flower wreaths or necklaces).

Zoris: *(zor-eez)* Flat, thonged sandals usually made of straw, leather, or rubber.

Chapter Five

Aloha shirt: *(ah-low-hah* shirt*)* A loose-fitting man's Hawaiian shirt worn outside the pants. The garment is usually very colorful.

Axis: *(ak-sis)* The nations engaged against the Allied nations in World War II—Germany, Italy, and Japan.

Kabuki dolls: *(kuh-boo-kee* dolls*)* Dolls made up to look like the highly stylized Kabuki dancers of traditional Japanese drama.

Kihilis: *(kah-hee-leez)* An ancient Hawaiian emblem of royalty consisting of a staff or shaft, with one end looking somewhat like a big feather duster. A commoner seeing someone approaching carrying a kahili was required to lie face down so that the royal person would not be defiled by a commoner's shadow, gaze, or touch.

Koa: *(ko-ah)* A Hawaiian timber tree with crescent-shaped leaves and white flowers.

Lanai: *(lay-nay-ee)* A patio, porch, or balcony.

Lihue: *(lee-hoo-ee)* The small city that is the commercial and governing center of the Hawaiian island of Kauai. Lihue is also the site of the island's main commercial airport.

Muumuu: *(moo-oo-moo-oo)* A loose, colorful dress or gown frequently worn by women in Hawaii. This word is sometimes mispronounced "moo-moo."

Papaya: *(puh-pie-yuh)* A large, oblong, yellow fruit grown in tropical areas.

Petroglyphs: *(pe-truh-glifs)* Prehistoric drawings or carvings on rocks. In Hawaii, the term refers to crude drawings on rocks probably made by early Polynesian visitors to the islands.

Shoji screen: *(show-jee screen)* A wooden-framed paper screen, often decorated, used as a wall, partition, or sliding door in Japanese homes.

Chapter Six

Kiawe: *(kee-ah-vay)* A thorny tree that can grow as tall as a house.

Chapter Nine

Buddhist: *(bood-uhst)* A person who follows the religion that grew out of the teaching of Gautama

Buddha.

Dozo: *(doe-zoe)* Japanese for "please."

Hai: *(hi)* Japanese for "yes."

Kimono: *(ka-moh-nah)* A long robe with wide sleeves traditionally worn with a broad sash as an outer garment by the Japanese.

Monkeypod: An ornamental tropical tree that has clusters of flowers, sweet pods eaten by cattle, and wood used in carving.

Samurai: *(sam-ah-rye)* Part of the Japanese aristocracy.

Chapter Thirteen

Holoku: *(hoe-low-koo)* A dress or gown with a train worn by Hawaiian women.